Jean Drummond Barrie was born in Sussex, raised in London after the War and has lived all her married life in Kent with her husband. She has one married daughter. Her interests include religion and her hobbies include reading, writing poetry, films and quilting.

Dedication

To my husband, Barrie, who has been my rock, and dear friend, Marion, without whom this book would never have been published.

Jean Drummond Barrie

FLAME

AUSTIN MACAULEY PUBLISHERS™
LONDON • CAMBRIDGE • NEW YORK • SHARJAH

A CIP catalogue record for this title is available from the British Library.

ISBN 9781788784122 (Paperback)
ISBN 9781788784139 (Hardback)
ISBN 9781788784146 (E-Book)

www.austinmacauley.com

First Published (2018)
Austin Macauley Publishers Ltd™
25 Canada Square
Canary Wharf
London
E14 5LQ

Acknowledgements

To all at Austin Macauley publishers for making this book possible.

Chapter 1

High Tor was a beautiful area in the Scottish Highlands. The land was owned by the McGregor family. It comprised of several thousands of acres in size and was made up of moorland, hills, valleys and rivers. High Tor House was the family home, a lovely old manor set on top of a hill, showing stunning views in all directions. A number of farms were also part of the McGregor estate and these, along with the hunting, fishing and shooting trips they ran, kept High Tor in good financial shape, but now it had all changed. It is the year 1943 and for the past four years, war has raged over Europe. High Tor House and its lands were taken over to aid the war effort two years ago. Hamish and Isla McGregor (the current Laird and his wife) had moved out and now lived in their town house in Inverness. Their son, Rory, though, had insisted on remaining. He had volunteered for the Army at the outbreak of war but been refused as he was needed to oversee the farms. They were essential for food production. At first, Rory had been angry, as he had watched his farm workers rushing to join up, but when the General and his men had turned up, forcing his parents out of their home and taking over the moors, he had been glad to be here and make a stand. He had insisted his presence was needed for the production of food. After a number of meetings, it was finally agreed he could stay in the flat over the stables, originally used by their head groom. Their lovely horses had gone at the outbreak of war. Rory split the flat into an office, sitting room and sleeping quarters and though cramped, it did work.

The officer in charge of the House was simply known as the General, no surname; in fact, everything there was secret. However, Rory and the General had grown into an uneasy understanding, a wary respect for each other. Soon after, it was agreed that Rory was to stay at High Tor, the General had insisted he sign the official secrets act and had listed him as a civilian driver.

"That should keep London happy," he told Rory, "They won't evict you for any reason now, at a later date." Rory thanked him.

For months now, Rory had watched the comings and goings closely. He continually wondered what they were doing in his home and out on the moors. Everything was hush-hush. If he met any of the soldiers and tried to pass the time of day, he was totally blanked. The General had made it clear that there could be no contact between the civilians and them. *Who were 'them'?* Rory fretted. Rory was also refused permission to go inside the house. There were sentries everywhere and then one day, Rory heard explosions out on the moors. *What were they doing?*

Rory was twenty-five years old, well educated at Oxford and well-travelled. He was tall, lean and strong, with dark hair worn longer than was acceptable and had dark sensual eyes. He knew High Tor would one day be his and he loved every inch of it. He worked hard to learn all aspects of work undertaken at High Tor, helping out on the farms and out on the moors with the hunting, shooting and fishing parties. He had felled trees with the forestry commission and culled deer with his gamekeeper. He had also studied accountancy and shadowed his dad on business trips. He wanted to be prepared for when the time came. Now, his dad was living in Inverness, there were times when he had to take over already.

Rory had one constant companion, his Border Collie bitch, Bonny. She had been the smallest in a litter of pups on one of the farms and the farmer had rejected her. He was going to send her out to be someone's pet, not waste time on training her as a working dog. Rory had taken her on and never regretted it. His life was often spent alone, and Bonny filled that empty space. The two were inseparable.

Rory had one other close friend, Callum Brody. They were the same age and had grown up together. Callum's father had been Game Keeper on High Tor as his father before him. Sadly, he had died suddenly two years ago, and Callum had taken on the position, as expected. The two of them had travelled to school together, spent holidays tramping the moors, hunting and fishing with Callum's dad. They had gone to join up together and been rejected together; Callum because of a back injury he had suffered in his teens when he'd fallen whilst climbing with Rory. Rory would never forget that day or the dramatic journey by ambulance to the hospital. The two shared a love of High Tor, of the wildlife and the solitude it offered out in wild places. They were close, shared confidences and worries. Callum lived at Beacon Farm with his mother and younger sister, Caitlin. The farm was a second home to Rory and he spent many happy hours there.

Today, the two met up at one of the farms. Callum had excitedly told Rory that twin calves had been born two days earlier and he just had to see them. He and Callum stood leaning over a gate, watching the calves. They brought smiles to both their faces. Eventually, they had to leave and go their separate ways; Callum to collect essential stores and Rory to head into Inverness to see his parents. On the way, he picked up Caitlyn, who wanted to see a friend in Inverness. Rory and Caitlyn were getting engaged the following weekend. Her mother, Morag, was hosting a gathering to celebrate at Beacon Farm. Rory was happy with the arrangement; although, he admitted to some reservations. Firstly, Caitlyn was young at eighteen, too young he sometimes wondered. For himself, he admitted this was no passionate affair, yet Caitlyn was a beautiful brunette, with long dark hair and deep brown eyes. She was no longer the little kid who had followed Callum and himself around everywhere up at High Tor. He had always understood why, life was often very lonely in the wilds and she was the only girl. Even so, he had been surprised when recently she had admitted to falling in love with him. In fact, he'd been pleased, as his parents had been hinting; it was time he considered marriage and who more suitable than Caitlyn? She had grown up on the moors and understood the loneliness, knew the isolation in winters, when they were snowed in. Even better, her mother was within easy reach, so she would have help when their children arrived. Overall, Rory was pleased with the thought of marriage to Caitlyn. He looked forward to having her in his life, in his bed and thoughts of a son and heir excited him.

Hamish and Isla welcomed their son and Caitlyn warmly. Isla gave Caitlyn a gentle hug before hugging Rory. She was so pleased to see them both. Hamish was eager to hear news of High

Tor; he and Rory disappeared into the sitting room whilst Isla and Caitlyn headed for the kitchen to discuss the engagement party.

Caitlyn told her, "Mum has everything covered. My friends from work have all accepted the invitations and Rory has invited all the Estate workers."

"It will be a good gathering then," Isla nodded. "We've not had any parties since the war began."

"People keep asking me when we'll wed but Rory refuses to set a date. He says we should wait until the war ends so he can take me straight to the House as his bride," Caitlyn complained.

Isla commiserated, yet understood, "That has been the McGregor tradition for a long time and Rory believes in the old family traditions. He can be stubborn too, Caitlyn, so I doubt he'll change his mind once it's made up." She smiled at the young girl, "We'll just have to hope the war ends soon."

Caitlyn pouted, "Not if I can help it! I want to get married soon. I've started making enquiries about a spring wedding."

"Well, I have to say, Rory won't be pushed, but if you can persuade him, who knows?" She was surprised and a little concerned by Caitlyn's announcement. It was already October! She changed the subject, "Put the kettle on love, we'll have our tea." She bustled about putting out cups and saucers, before filling plates with sandwiches, scones and cake. "This is such a come down. When I remember the high teas we had at High Tor before the war, this looks pitiful, but as we're constantly told, there is a war on!"

"Mum sent you some eggs and cheese, Isla, from the farm," Caitlyn told her. "They are in here." She handed over a bag and Isla thanked her gratefully.

In the sitting room, Hamish was cross examining Rory on the latest happenings at High Tor. He missed his home far more than he admitted. After asking about some of his employees, he wanted to know, "What's the latest with the House?"

Rory shrugged, "Things are as secretive as ever, Dad. I'm sure they are training spies or some such. I can hear language classes being held in the house and fire arm training out on the moors. I've done a couple of driving jobs recently. I drove a soldier to the station last week and got the impression he'd failed the course he was on. He was obviously out of it and seemed shocked and upset."

"If they are training the chaps that go out to assist the French Resistance, then they are very brave men," Hamish decided. "They are sent out to sabotage, even kill, and they often lose their lives."

"Not just chaps Dad. I've seen a couple of women up there too," Rory told him.

"My goodness, I didn't know that—women, eh? God help them!"

Rory nodded slowly, his thoughts exactly. Hamish then asked, concerned, "These driving jobs you do, there's nothing dangerous in them, I hope?"

"No Dad. In fact, there aren't many of them. I just do the odd ones to look good on the General's records. I am listed as a driver, after all."

"How is the General?" wondered Hamish. Actually, he didn't particularly like the man who had the power to evict him from his home.

"He was well the last time I saw him," Rory knew how his dad felt. "He is actually okay, you know Dad. He's just doing a hard job, I'd guess."

"Mm, if you say so. How is Caitlyn?" Hamish wasn't at all happy about this engagement. Isla was excited about it but as far as he could see, Rory wasn't head over heels in love with the girl. Caitlyn was still young, she loved the bright lights of town and the parties here. He thought her moody and selfish, not like her brother. He had watched Callum and Caitlyn grow up with Rory and Callum was different. He fully approved of him, agreed he was older but he was hardworking and reliable. He, sadly, believed Rory was being manipulated by Caitlyn into this engagement, but what could he do?

"Caitlyn is fine. She'll be in with Mum a minute. She is staying in town with friends tonight."

"Then you'll have a lonely journey home. Why not stay here with us tonight?" Hamish invited.

Rory thought about it, was tempted, in fact, but declined, "I'd love to Dad, but I left Bonny in one of the stables. I'll need to see to her tonight."

Hamish understood that, "Then come another time, we don't see enough of you and that flat can't be comfortable."

"It's not that bad Dad. It's nice and warm, just a bit small after the House," he grinned. That was an understatement.

Hamish returned to Caitlyn, he couldn't help it. He was concerned. "Are you sure you want to marry Caitlyn? I need to ask you, son, then I'll shut up."

"Oh, Dad really, I'm twenty-five, surely old enough to decide these things for myself," Rory flushed, embarrassed.

"That's not an answer. Okay, I'll not push you, but listen to me. Caitlyn is young, she still enjoys the social life here in Inverness and I'm not sure she'll settle to life out on the moors. Please be sure, marriage is easy enough to fall into, but if it's a mistake, it's damn hard to get out of," he sighed. "There, I've had my say. I'll shut up."

Rory was acutely embarrassed. Deep inside, he suspected his dad was pointing out what he already knew. He was simply settling for Caitlyn because she was there. It was no love match on his part, but Caitlyn wanted him, and he wanted children. It was all very convenient. However, he couldn't tell his dad this.

Hamish waited for Rory to insist he loved Caitlyn. When he didn't, he was even more concerned. If only Rory could find a woman to rouse fierce passions in him, just like Isla had done to him all those years ago. He sighed, the silence stretching uncomfortably. He'd done his best to get Rory out into the world, appreciating how lonely his life had been growing up on the moors. He'd seen him well educated at Oxford and sent him travelling for a year around Europe. He'd spent time in France and Germany, learning the language in each. It was so hard now to have to sit back and let him make a mistake over Caitlyn. Hamish was very relieved when Isla and Caitlyn brought in the tea tray, laden with afternoon tea.

Chapter 2

Later, that day Rory took Caitlyn to her friend's home, where she would stay for the weekend. The two girls worked together on a magazine, Caitlyn did part time because of the journey into Inverness. Unbeknown to Rory, the girls planned to spend the time in Edinburgh, not Inverness, at a party organised by Canadian soldiers, based there.

For once, Rory was glad to get away from his parents and to be alone in his flat. His head was still buzzing with his dad's warning over Caitlyn and he'd have found it hard to spend any more time listening to him. The fact it bothered him only proved, there was truth in his dad's words and he needed to consider them. On one side, he needed to marry if he was to produce an heir. He knew Caitlyn well, including her faults. She was young, could be selfish and enjoyed a social life. Would she settle to married life, out on the moors? She swore she loved him and would be happy married to him. He was also aware, her social standing would rise as his wife and would ensure plenty of engagements, both business and charities. Would these be enough to keep her happy? Finally, coward that he was, how could he get out of it now, (not that he wanted to) with the engagement party next weekend? Common-sense though assured him, an engagement didn't mean actual marriage, did it? He would go ahead with the engagement but defer the marriage until after the war. Caitlyn might not like it, she was keen to seal the deal, but on this he would stand firm. Happy at last with his decision he took Bonny out for a late night walk. He loved it out here after dark, walking below a million stars. Only one thing disturbed his peace, the number of sentries out patrolling the grounds. Still, Bonny was happy with lots of exciting smells, mice and rabbits to chase. Rory was relaxed at last. Nothing could take away the contentment, he felt in his home surroundings.

It was on Tuesday morning of the following week that Rory had a telephone call from the General.

"Good morning, McGregor. I have a special driving job for you this evening, if you're willing. This one is different though, totally risk free I assure you, taking a person to a secret location. I'm stuck for a driver. My men have no wish to go out onto the moors after dark and to tell the truth, I doubt they'd even find the place. I thought of you."

"Tonight is fine by me, sir," Rory agreed.

"This is top secret, McGregor, never to be spoken about, do you understand?" the General spoke gruffly.

"Yes sir, I understand," Rory was interested now. This sounded exciting.

"Good man. Be at the Lodge gates at twenty thirty, a car and person will be there. I'll give you the co-ordinates now, so you can plan a route." He read out the figures required, and Rory wrote them down, before repeating them back. The General confirmed they were right then continued, "Please don't ask any questions of the person concerned and forget everything you see after tonight. Understand?"

"Yes General, I understand. I'll be at the gates at twenty thirty."

"I'm grateful to you, McGregor. Thank you," he hung up.

Intrigued by the conversation, Rory got out his map box and searched the Highlands for the co-ordinates. There was nothing at the destination, just a long valley with a river running through it. It was in a very remote part of the Highlands and Rory doubted, it was even part of High Tor land. Well, this got even more interesting. No wonder none of the soldiers wanted to do it, he grinned, whereas he was thrilled, and challenged to take it on! It wouldn't be an easy journey, especially at night and in pitch darkness. He studied the map more closely, working out a route, changing it until he was certain, he'd made the right choice. It should get him there in about an hour and a half. A shiver of excitement went through him as he wondered what tonight would bring.

Rory called Bonny and he took her for an early run before feeding her and settling her in one of the stables with fresh hay and water. With Bonny sorted for the night, Rory made himself a meal before heading for the Lodge gates, arriving a little early. He gave the impression of being calm and in control but inside his heart was beating a tattoo. This was top secret and he had no idea what to expect!

Minutes after he arrived, a land rover pulled up and Rory nodded. A good choice considering the roads where they were going were often mere dirt tracks. A soldier got out of the driving seat and approached Rory. "Mr McGregor, sir?"

"Yes," Rory stepped forward.

"Here you are, sir," he handed over the keys and Rory got into the car. He was aware of a figure in the back and nodded, "Good evening," before firing up the engine.

The night was cold, the roads narrow and hard to negotiate in places, making the going rough and slow. Rory drove on, his passenger silent until about half an hour into the journey he heard a noise from the back and slowed the car to a crawl.

"Please stop the car," he was told. Rory's instinct went into overdrive!

"Why would I stop out here?" he asked in disbelief.

"I'm going to be sick," the man told him, "Please!"

Rory pulled up, still wary. Was this a trap?

The man fell out of the car and Rory heard retching. Next moment, a loud groan filled the silent night and more sickness followed. By now, Rory was concerned and he got out of the car. "If you get back in the car, I'll take you back to High Tor," he decided.

"No—no—I have to go," the man insisted.

"Go where?" Rory wondered, forgetting he'd been told not to ask questions.

"Please continue," the man got back in the car. Rory shrugged and did as he was asked. He drove on.

Finally, the valley was before them and Rory stared in disbelief. Here and there a glimmer of light lit up a building, a warehouse and a hanger. There were vehicles too he saw as his eyes took it all in. Unbelievably, in front of him was a small aircraft. He'd arrived at an airfield

Suddenly, a figure approached the car. "We're cleared for take-off. Where are the packages?"

"In the boot, there's only two, one heavy," the man replied before stepping out of the car, only to collapse on the ground, groaning.

Rory leapt out and stood over him. Now, he could see his passenger was a young man, maybe twenty. "What's wrong?" he demanded.

"Stomach pains, bad," the man groaned. He was as white as a sheet, sweating and doubled up on the ground.

"What's going on?" the second man demanded, having obviously loaded the boxes onto the plane.

"He's sick," Rory told him. "What happens now?"

"Don't ask me! I'm just the pilot stupid enough to risk my neck, flying them into France." He looked more closely, "He can't go in that state. Best take him back."

"I have to go!" the man suddenly dragged himself up, "Those goods are desperately needed. There will be people waiting, risking their lives and I have documents. Let me get on board."

The pilot took his arm and looked him over, "Sorry mate, trips off. I can't take you in that state."

"But I have to get these things out there! You'll have me back in no time," the agent pleaded.

"What's so important in those boxes?" Rory asked. This was all exciting stuff!

"Radios, medical supplies, guns, whatever the Resistance wants, we try to get it out there," the agent was desperate and sick and had no idea he was giving away classified information. "I just have to go," he added.

The pilot shook his head, "I'm not prepared to take you. You'll be a danger to me and the Resistance in your state, not to mention putting your own life in danger. You need to get to hospital."

Rory couldn't help curiosity getting the better of him, "How does this work then? Do you simply fly out and hand the boxes over and come back?"

"There's nothing simple about it," the pilot told him, "If it goes well, then yes we land, hand over and fly back. But, if no one is waiting to meet us, the agent gets out and waits and if he's lucky, he returns next trip. Some never return," he finished.

"Is that true?" Rory asked the agent.

"I've only been out once and yes, I came back the same night."

"Are you thinking of coming for a trip?" the pilot asked Rory, grinning wickedly.

That had been exactly what Rory had been thinking, but he had concerns for the agent. "What about him?"

"I'll radio in, before we leave. Someone from over there will come and see him," he pointed towards the buildings.

"I'm not trained for this," Rory admitted, his heart thumping. His head was telling him not to be so stupid.

"It is up to you. We go now, or I abandon the trip. Make up your mind," the pilot insisted.

"You said you'd bring me back?" Rory hedged.

"Only if it goes to plan, there are no guarantees in this business. If not, I leave you in enemy territory," the pilot spoke harshly.

Rory looked again at the sick man. He knew it was impossible for him to go. "You mentioned documents?" he asked.

The man drew a large envelope from his coat, "Here, these ones. Are you seriously considering going?" he gasped. "You must realise how dangerous it is out there. At least I've been trained." He again doubled up in pain, Rory noticed.

Rory took the envelope, "Then wish me luck, will you?" he smiled, "I hope you'll feel better soon," he turned to the pilot, "Let's go." He headed for the plane.

The pilot indicated a seat, "Strap yourself in and listen to me carefully. Once in the air; we do not speak. As soon as I land, you have two minutes to open the door and unload the boxes. If no one is there to meet us, you get out and hide them and yourself, until someone turns up. I will keep the engine running all the time, we are on the ground. After two minutes I take off, with or without you." He sounded harsh and Rory swallowed hard, before the pilot continued more softly, "I have to get the plane away or we'll be picked up on radar and everyone caught. Now this is your last chance, do you wish to go?" Rory nodded, he had said he'd go and he'd not change his mind now. Next moment they were in the air.

Half an hour later, Rory was having severe doubts about this outing. It had sounded simple enough back on the ground, now he questioned what on earth he was doing. The plane was hitting turbulence and being buffeted about crazily. Rory wondered, if they would even reach their destination alive! Suddenly the plane banked steeply, turned and headed for the ground. Now, Rory was praying like he'd never prayed before, 'Please let someone be there to meet us'. He wanted to go home, he'd never been so afraid, he admitted. The landing was hard and shook him up badly. Next moment, he realised they were stationery. He opened the door. It was dark outside as his eyes searched for someone, anyone! There was no one. He unloaded the first box, then the second, still no one came. As he stepped out of the plane, his whole body was shaking.

The pilot called softly "Sorry mate. Hide yourself until someone comes for you." He revved up the engine and Rory watched horrified as the plane took off and disappeared. He stood transfixed. He was alone in France, behind enemy lines and terrified. He had to hide, his mind insisted. He dragged a box across to some dense bushes and pushed it deep inside. The second box, he moved further away and also hid it in bushes. This time, he pushed the documents inside the rough sacking that covered the box. Now to hide himself, he decided and memories of times he'd spent out on the moors with Callum came back. Callum's dad had taught them well, "If you are caught out in the open, find a hollow and cover yourselves with foliage." However, before he could move a twig cracked nearby and a voice speaking German, demanded, "Put your hands above your head" and next moment a rifle prodded him in the back.

Chapter 3

Yvette sat high up in a tree, watching the scene unfold below her. They, the Resistance had been betrayed again! This was not the first time. The Germans were here ahead of them again and she'd been forced to abort the operation to save her fellow workers. Her anger was boiling over. Brave men risked their lives to get supplies to them, just like the man below being surrounded by Germans. Well, no more, she decided, there would be no more drops in her area until the traitor in their midst was caught.

Yvette watched carefully. The Germans hadn't found the supplies the agent had hidden so carefully. All was not lost, if they could recover them later. So much depended on getting them into the hands of the Resistance, they were desperately needed.

Yvette was a Resistance Leader, her code name Flame. She was twenty-two years old, small at five three tall, blonde haired and blue eyes yet nothing about her was remotely doll like. She was athletic, strong and wiry. Even more so, she was brave and clever too, working as an accountant during the day. Her earlier actions had quickly raised her to cell leader of a small group responsible for the plane drops in her area. She was a fully trained radio operator, (hence her code name), spoke fluent German and had passed self-defence, first aid, gun training and how to kill. Up until now, her little group had enjoyed plenty of success. Carefully planned operations had run like clock-work, until now. Twice now the Germans had arrived at the precise time a drop was due, and two agents had been caught. Flame felt guilty, it was her who had arranged the drops and led the men into danger, if not death. She had to stop any more men flying into danger.

The Germans had searched the man and now turned him around to handcuff him as she saw. Suddenly, it seemed as if the man stared straight at her. It was the strangest sensation, unnerving her as heat flooded through her body. The man was tall, she noticed, strength was obvious in the way he held himself. He was showing no sign of fear, but surely, he was afraid? He had dark hair she sensed rather than saw as it was dark, and she couldn't be sure. She had the strongest yearning to meet him, learn more about him. She must be crazy she decided, as the Germans marched him away.

"I'm sorry," Flame whispered into the night air, as if he could hear her, she scorned herself.

Flame stayed in her tree a while longer. She was cold and stiff, but too afraid to move too soon, in case the Germans had left a guard. Finally, she slid down silently and breathed a sigh of relief as all was quiet as she made her way out of the woods.

Flame made her way to a local farm, owned by one of her cell members, Yves. She was warmly welcomed and given tea and toast, whilst she explained what had happened after the men had left. "We need to get the supplies as soon as possible," she told him. He agreed and offered to use his truck.

Later that day, Wednesday, Flame was alone in her flat above an outbuilding, on Yves farm. She had been living here ever since she joined the Resistance. She was delighted at the success they had snatched from the jaws of disaster. The boxes had now been dealt with, the supplies ready for distribution to people waiting for them. It had taken her no time to find the envelope Rory had hidden and she now settled down to decipher the message, it contained. What she read sent shivers down her spine. Other cells had also been infiltrated, agents and workers betrayed, some known to have been executed already. It warned Flame of the danger she was in, well she lived with danger every day, but this was a new deadly threat to her. Someone she knew and trusted was betraying them all. Anger boiled again as she vowed somehow, she would find out who they were and deal with them! She had not killed so far, but she'd do it, in a moment, once she knew who it was.

Flame checked her watch. It was nearly time for her radio slot. She took out her radio from its secret hiding place, got out her code books and wrote out her report. When her time came, she informed London the supplies had been collected but the agent arrested. She asked for all drops to her to be suspended until the traitor was caught. Now she waited, afraid. Being on air too long risked her position being discovered. Her call sign came back immediately, and she wrote out the coded message, acknowledged it and shut down. She replaced her radio and settled down to decode the message. What she read stunned her. It was unbelievable. "The agent who arrived is not a trained operative. His name is Rory McGregor, a VIP. He must be returned immediately. Notify us when he's ready to leave."

Flame read it through again, in amazement. This man, Rory McGregor, wasn't an agent? Then what the hell was he doing on that plane? He wasn't trained but what information did he have? Did he know about her cell? Oh God, he was already in German hands! London wanted him back but what was she supposed to do? She had never rescued anyone from German hands. Agents who were caught knew they were on their own. They came here knowing the risks they took. Flame paced up and down. This man, Rory, was totally unprepared for German interrogation methods. He was in danger, as was everyone, because of him! He must be important if London wanted him back, she mused, and were prepared to organise a return trip! However, it seemed it fell to her to rescue him. How on earth was she going to do that?

Flame made herself a cup of tea and tried to calm down. She needed a clear head. She looked back to the previous agent caught here. She had tried to find out what had happened to him. All she had been able to find out was he'd been held in a police cell in Villenue, the Germans having taken over the police station there. After about a week, he'd been transferred to Paris Gestapo. She shuddered. It was accepted everywhere, that it was best to die first rather than be sent there! Would the same procedure be used for Rory? If so, with luck they could have a few days left to get him out. Flame knew Villenue well. It had been her home town. She had lived there from the age of ten with her adopted parents. This gave her the first glimmer of a plan. When the Germans invaded France, her parents had tried to escape, taking her with them. However, they had been separated in the crowds and Flame had made the decision to return to her home. She had been nearly eighteen at the time. However, her home was in ruins after an apparent gas leak and explosion. With nowhere to live, Flame had cleared a way into the cellar, salvaged some furniture and stayed there until she joined the Free French. Now, her thoughts turned to the cellar. It was only a couple of blocks from the police station. If they could get Rory out of the police station they could be in the cellar underground before the Germans had time to organise a search party. The biggest problem was still how to get him out!

Finally, Flame decided she could do nothing tonight. She cleared all her paperwork away, safely out of sight and prepared for bed. Her final thoughts were of the man she had seen, standing straight before his captures, a brave man who had showed them no fear. A man who had looked straight at her it seemed. She'd do anything in her power to save him.

On Thursday morning, Flame went to find Yves. He was busy in the milking parlour. She smiled a greeting, "I know how busy you are, but have you time for an emergency meeting at Gervaise's shop?"

"Yes, of course. What's the emergency? Is it our traitor?"

"Something else has cropped up for now, but we'll have to discuss that sometime too. What time can you be free?" Flame asked.

"Give me an hour to finish milking my ladies," he smiled at her.

A little over an hour later, Yves lorry pulled up outside Gervaise's shop in Villenue. Gervaise owned and ran the green grocers shop. He was married, with two school age children. Flame and Yves entered singly, each bought something and left, only to slip around to the back of the shop, where Gervaise waited to let them in to a back room. He greeted them quickly and asked, "This must be something urgent. What is it Flame, I can only spare a few moments"?

"I understand Gervaise. Thanks for seeing us." They settled around a table and Flame quickly explained. "We need to get him out. Has anyone any ideas?

"I'm sure, you are right about him being in the police station. They will keep him there until an escort comes to take him to the Gestapo," Gervaise nodded, "Could we get him out of there, by being the escort?"

"We'd need uniforms, paperwork and transport," Yves summed up.

"And all in a hurry, he won't be there long, I'd guess," Flame sighed.

"I could contact the Forger about papers. I'd need the man's name," Gervaise offered and Flame gave it to him.

"Do we know how long they will take?" Flame fretted, but Gervaise shrugged, "Who knows?"

"What about uniforms?" Yves asked again. "And transport."

"We could use my van, but we'd have to park it well away from the Germans. It's nothing like their vans," Gervaise offered.

"We could go at night, so it wouldn't be seen so well. As for uniforms, could I be fixed up and go in alone? A female escort will give us the element of surprise, especially at night," Flame wondered.

"Maybe, that would work. Is your German good enough?" Yves asked. "As for a woman's uniform, I'll ask around other cells. Do you have a grey skirt?"

"Yes, I have. How long is all this going to take? We can't risk going in, if he's already been moved on," Flame frowned.

"Have you thought where to take him, if we get him out?" this from Gervaise.

"Yes, I have thought of somewhere in Villeneue. Hopefully, it will only be for a short time," Flame told him.

"Right, I suggest you come back here tomorrow and we'll see what we've got," Gervaise stood up, "I really must get back in the shop."

Flame agreed, "This is quite a challenge. We've not done anything like this before. I wish we had more time to plan, but we don't."

The three slipped away quietly, their heads buzzing with the task that lay ahead.

On Friday morning, Flame arrived at Gervaise's first and waited impatiently in the back room. Yves finally arrived apologising, he'd found a sick cow and had to see to it.

Gervaise got straight to the point, "The paperwork is in hand and they will be ready by lunch time on Saturday."

"I have been promised a female officers jacket and cap from Jacq's cell," Yves told her. "I'll pick them up this afternoon."

"Oh, that's great," Flame beamed at them. It had been a tremendous effort by them both, "You've both done a great job, so Saturday night we should be ready for the rescue." She thought for a moment, "I suggest just you and me, Gervaise, you to stay outside the police station, ready for a quick get a way, whilst I go in. Yves, will you wait here at the shop for Gervaise's return? If things go wrong, you take over the cell and let London know we tried to get McGregor out." Yves nodded, he understood. Flame continued, "Have I covered everything? Have you any questions?"

"I have one Flame. Where are you taking the man once we rescue him? I need to know for petrol," this from Gervaise.

"Of course, it is a ruined building, about a mile from the police station. If all goes well, we'll be safe underground before he's missed. I will guide you and once there, you drop us and go, Gervaise, don't hang around," she insisted.

Gervaise nodded, as if he would!

"That's everything then. We'll meet here tomorrow night at eleven and pray for a successful op!" Flame knew this was the riskiest thing any of them had attempted so far. Tomorrow night would decide if they'd pulled it off.

Chapter 4

Rory sat in the little cell all hope gone. He crossed off another square on the paper he'd prepared to keep track of the days. He made it on Saturday night. He'd been questioned each day but had mainly been left alone. The Germans were okay, he'd seen no violence so far and been given some food. The questions were monotonous, the same ones over and over. He'd given his name, told them he came from Scotland, but couldn't answer anything else, simply because he didn't know. Still they asked for names, places, who was meeting him? He couldn't answer. Rory spoke fluent French and understood German, thanks to his dad insisting he learnt both languages well before he left for his travels, all those years ago. However, he never let on to the Germans. He stumbled over his answers in French to them and looked blank when they spoke German. He passed many an hour listening to his captors chatting in German. Today, he sensed they were losing interest in him and finally, he was told what to expect. Paris was going to send for him and the dreaded word Gestapo was mentioned for the first time. He'd been shocked and trembled afterwards, but then accepted he had no one to blame but himself. No one had forced him onto that plane, he'd volunteered, so now he had to face the consequences. He also realised just how brave the men training at High Tor were. They trained in extreme practises ready to face what he himself was facing. Well, he now had to dig deep and find the courage himself to get through this. He was determined that he would not feel sorry for himself, nor show any fear to his captors.

Rory did regret his spur of the moment decision to get on that plane, of course he did. He didn't want to die. He was deeply saddened for what he was doing to his parents. They would be horrified to learn what he'd done, especially his mother. And he worried about Bonny, shut up in the stables. Would anyone find

27

her and look after her? He knew the anguish and pain, he was causing to everyone and he silently begged forgiveness. He then sat up, shocked, he'd not thought, tonight was the engagement party! He'd not given a thought about it or Caitlyn. It was an uncomfortable feeling to realise Caitlyn meant so little to him, he'd forgotten all about her. He shook his head, what did it matter now? He had to face reality, he was never going to get out of this alive, never see his family or Scotland again. The end was inevitable. He'd have to accept it.

The guards were quiet now and he checked his watch. It had gone eleven, so they were probably settling down for the night. Funny, now he faced the end of his life he felt he didn't need to sleep, which was surprising as he'd not slept properly since his arrest. He lay back on the hard-wooden bench that served as a bed and tucked his hands behind his head. For the first time since his arrest he felt calm. He had finally reached a state of acceptance and was no longer fighting the situation he was in.

He must have dozed off for a sudden flurry of activity had him wide awake. He couldn't see anything from his cell, but he could hear quite clearly and understand every word.

"I am here to remove your prisoner, McGregor to Paris." It was a woman speaking. A woman was here to take him to Paris?

A soldier was objecting strongly, "Not releasing him at this time of night".

The woman again, "Please hand him over, I've had a hell of a journey getting here. You have my name, rank and the correct documents for his release."

There were more objections and now another soldier was joining in. Rory gathered this hand over was most unusual, they should have been informed of the woman's arrival by telephone. He held his breath. He had no idea what awaited him in Paris, but he was sure it wouldn't be pleasant. Flickers of fear coursed through his brain.

Next moment, a soldier opened his cell door. "Out, you're going to Paris," he told him. He waited for Rory to put on his jacket before handcuffing him. Rory's first impression of the woman was how short she was. She had dark hair, swept up under her cap. Glasses covered her eyes and her uniform was far from flattering. She grabbed his arm firmly, "Move!" she yelled, pushing him towards the door. The Germans stood back confused but so was Rory after days confined inside. Outside it was dark and he stared around. A few yards away a van waited, engine's running. Again, the woman pushed him roughly,

"Get in the van!" she demanded, but this time she spoke French. Rory was lost, he stared at her, hesitating. What was going on? "For God's sake, get in," she cried desperately, "Unless you want us to leave you here?" Rory leapt into the van and they were away. No more words were spoken until almost immediately the van stopped again. The woman turned to Rory. "Get out," she told him, and he slid out again. "Go Gervaise!" she cried, and the van disappeared. Rory was in total shock by now and again he stared at her.

"This way," she took his arm gently this time. "Follow me closely." It was very dark, no lights that he could see, blackout he supposed. The woman led him over some rubble to the side of a ruined building. He followed blindly, what else could he do? When she stopped she lifted a paving slab to one side and told him, "Get in." This time Rory stopped dead and demanded, "What is this, what is happening to me?" in a voice thick with fear.

"Too many questions, I'm here to save your life. Please get in," she insisted, then relented, "I'll follow, never fear. I have to replace the slab."

For some unknown reason Rory believed her. Some instinct told him to trust her. He moved to the hole and as he passed her she shone a torch, so he could see. The entrance was small as he squeezed himself into it. However, once inside he found a flight of stairs downwards. Flame followed, and the torch showed him a large cellar sparsely furnished. She went to a table and lit a candle, before turning off the torch and smiled at him, "I must save the battery." From the table she took a skeleton key, "Let's try this," she struggled with the handcuffs and eventually they fell off.

"Thanks," Rory mumbled.

"My pleasure, well, that went well, even if I do say so myself," she grinned, her eyes sparkling, "You can relax now Rory, you are safe here."

"You know my name?" Rory gasped. Of course she did, she'd used it at the police station, hadn't she?

"Yes, Mr Rory McGregor. London radioed about you. Oh! And my code name's Flame."

"Pleased to meet you Flame and my thanks for rescuing me," Rory smiled for the first time in days. "I do hope London spoke well of me?"

"Actually, they didn't seem very pleased with you," she admitted. "Let's make ourselves comfortable," she indicated a wooden chair, then lit a primus stove, boiled some water and made him a weak cup of tea. "Sorry, I had no time to get milk." There were two wooden chairs by the table and Flame joined him. Across the end of the cellar, there was a bed and a battered chest of drawers. Rory was taking it all in slowly.

"This place?" he asked, afraid to pry.

"This house was my home, years ago but as you can see it was badly damaged in a gas explosion. This cellar is ideal as my bolt hole. It's no hotel for you but I can guarantee you'll be safe down here."

Rory nodded, "I see, so, are you Resistance?" he wondered.

Flame raised her eyes heavenward, "If I'm not, then you are in big trouble mate!" she laughed. "Sorry, I shouldn't laugh. London said you aren't one of us. Can you tell me how you came to be on that plane?"

Rory nodded, getting on the plane seemed a lifetime away to him now. "I was asked to drive this man—the agent?" he wondered, and she nodded, "Well, the agent to the airstrip but he was taken seriously ill and the pilot refused to take him. I offered to take his place, as I expected to simply hand over the supplies and fly home again. It didn't turn out quite like that," he grinned.

"What a mess!" Flame exclaimed, "No wonder London got in a flap over you. What did you tell the Germans when they questioned you?"

Rory suddenly realised these weren't idle questions, he was being interrogated. Still Flame had just saved his life and he had nothing to hide. "I gave them my name and said I came from Scotland. I couldn't answer their questions. I know nothing about your set up here. I never told them I can speak French and understand German, I simply played dumb."

"Did they hurt you?" Flame asked.

"No, they didn't. I spent most of the time locked up. I was told my details had been sent to Paris and I would be collected. Can you tell me where in France we are?" Rory wondered.

"Villenue," she told him, "I'm glad we got you out in time," she meant every word. She was already finding him—interesting! He was every bit as attractive as she had thought him from her tree at the airstrip.

"Would you mind, if I changed out of this uniform? I'm afraid there's no privacy down here," Flame explained. She went to the back of the cellar and took some clothes out of the chest of drawers. Next moment to his amazement off came her glasses, followed by a wig! He was mesmerized. The uniform followed. Try as he might, to be a gentleman and not look, he simply stared. After all, he was just a man! Flame had the perfect body, curves in all the right places and the most glorious blonde hair. It fell in a golden cascade around her shoulders. She was stunning, beautiful, he gasped, unable to find the words he wanted. She slipped on a skirt and jumper, brushed out her hair and smiled at him as she returned to the table. Did she know, he'd stared at her? He flushed embarrassed, only now noticing her face was pink too.

Flame took a deep breath, settling her racing pulse, "There is a cold tap and basin in the corner and a chamber pot. I'll take it out and empty it each night."

Embarrassed all over again; Rory objected, "There's no need. I'm quite capable of seeing to it myself!"

"Oh, no way," Flame spoke sharply. "Whilst you are here you must remain down here out of sight. If you are caught, not only you but my cell will be in danger. You must do as I say from now on. Do you understand?"

Rory stared at her, she was some feisty woman! However, he nodded, "Yes, I understand Flame. I owe you and the others for saving my life. Believe me, I can't thank you enough. I won't do anything to put anyone in danger, I swear," he promised. "What happens now?" he wondered.

"I'm not sure. You are the first man we've rescued. I will get a message to London and tell them we have you here, the rest is up to them. They will arrange to get you back. For now, I suggest we should get some sleep." Suddenly, she seemed to hesitate.

The fact was Flame had suddenly found a flaw in her 'perfect' plan. There was only one, double bed in the cellar.

Chapter 5

Callum was the first person to miss Rory. It wasn't until Thursday morning, when Rory didn't turn up at Beacon Farm for a meeting that he felt something was wrong. His mother, Morag, tried to calm her son, "He's just been held up, he may be planning something for the party Saturday night."

"This meeting was arranged, to go over Jamie's plans for an extension on his farmhouse. Once Rory had seen the plans we were meeting Jamie. It's not like Rory, he'd have rung if he was held up," Callum worried.

"Well, I wanted to see him too," Caitlyn complained, "He hasn't even answered his phone. I want to discuss an idea I have for skiing after Christmas."

"Going away together? I think not Caitlyn. That won't happen until you are married!" Morag gasped.

"And when will that be, I'd like to know? All Rory says is we must wait until the war is over," Caitlyn cried.

"He's being sensible then, if you ask me," Callum snapped. "I cannot see you sitting here, night after night, waiting for your husband, should he be called up!" He was well aware of his sister's antics in Edinburgh whenever she could get away.

"You don't know anything Callum!" Caitlyn snapped and flounced out of the room.

Morag looked worried and Callum decided it was time to put his mother straight, "You do realise all this engagement lark is down to Caitlyn? Rory is all for waiting but not so Madam. I'll tell you something else, if she thinks she can get Rory to marry her before he's ready, she's going to be sorry." He thought deeply, "She's too young, Mum, and too fond of the high life. I can't say more."

"Are you sure about this Callum?" Morag looked horrified.

"I'm sure and now you know. Maybe, you could speak to her and do everyone a favour to stop her games," Callum insisted, "Oh, where is Rory? Cat says he's not answered her and I've been ringing the office without success. I'm going to drive over to the Stables," he decided.

The first thing Callum heard, when he pulled into the Stable yard, was Bonny crying piteously. He hurried over to the stable block and panic hit him. Poor Bonny was laying in the hay in deep distress. Her food and water bowls were empty. From the state she was in she had been here some time, he realised. He spoke quietly to her,

"Okay Bonny, I'm here. Let's get you out of there and find you some water." He opened the door as he spoke, and Bonny threw herself at him in sheer relief. He fetched her water from a yard tap and she drank thirstily. He stroked her gently. "What's been happening here then?" he asked, "Let's find you some food, shall we?" He led the way up to the flat. The door was unlocked but he knew somehow, that Rory wasn't going to be here, simply because of Bonny but he still he called out, "Hallo!" just in case Rory was ill, but there was no answer and the flat was empty. Now, he was terribly worried. He found some dog food in a cupboard and fed Bonny, who made short work of it. She then settled down beside Rory's desk, her favourite place.

Callum made a thorough search of the flat. Rory's bed hadn't been slept in, so he hadn't been here for at least twenty-four hours, or longer, he decided, judging by the state Bonny was in. He didn't know what to do. He filled a water bowl and told Bonny to stay where she was and went outside. Whilst he stood there a limousine pulled up outside the house and the General came out. Without thinking Callum ran across to him, "Please excuse me sir," he began, "have you seen Rory McGregor recently?"

"Mr McGregor? I'm sorry, I can't help you. I must go. I have a train to catch to London," he got in and the driver closed his door. Next moment, the car pulled away smoothly. For one split second, Callum swore he'd seen a flicker of fear in the man's eyes. He knew the man had lied. It was enough to shake Callum into action. He went back up to the office and searched Rory's desk diary. Rory should have had an appointment with a War Office official about vegetable figures, in Inverness yesterday.

He rang the number and asked if Rory had attended the meeting. He was told he hadn't and that Mr McGregor needed to rebook. Callum apologised, said the diary had been mislaid and hung up.

Now Callum was convinced something serious was going on here and there was nothing he could do alone. He rang Inverness again and spoke to Hamish. He explained briefly, and Hamish agreed to come straight over.

Callum was waiting nervously; when Hamish arrived. The two went straight to the office and Hamish began searching Rory's desk. He drew a blank, just as Callum had. When Callum told him about Bonny, Hamish turned white, "There's something going on here. Have you no idea where he could have gone?"

"None, oh, I wish I did. I just have this feeling—I know something's wrong," Callum admitted.

"When did you last see Rory?" Hamish asked.

"Monday night, we had a drink here and arranged to see Jamie today. I haven't seen or heard from him since. Oh, and Caitlyn said he hadn't been returning her calls either," Callum explained, "And as I said, he never turned up for a meeting yesterday. I don't think he's been here since Tuesday. One last thing, I saw the General outside earlier and asked him if he'd seen Rory. He said no, but I felt he knew something. That he was lying."

"If Rory is mixed up with the army, we'll only be told its top secret, but what on earth could Rory be doing for the army?"

"Well, he did say he drove for them sometimes," Callum admitted.

"Yes, he told me. Right, I'll go and have words with the General. Let's see what he says to me," Hamish stated firmly.

"He's not over there. He said he was off to London when I spoke to him."

"That settles it. I'm ringing the police, reporting Rory as a missing person," Hamish decided, "We have to do something. If he is mixed up with the Army, let the police find out." Hamish picked up the phone and asked for Inspector Harris, a man he knew from Rotary Club.

The Inspector came straight out to High Tor. He made lots of notes, took a statement from Callum and left again with Rory's desk diary. He said he'd organise a search but wouldn't be able to search High Tor land. The Army would be requested to do that. He'd also check local hospitals too. Callum insisted he wouldn't be out in the grounds without Bonny and she was shut up.

Hamish saw the Inspector drive away, before he asked Callum what needed doing business wise before he left. The two made some decisions and Hamish promised to come back tomorrow and help Callum with a meeting. Callum then decided to move into the flat to be there should Rory turn up and to answer the phone. He'd also take care of Bonny. Hamish then left for home, not looking forward to telling Isla Rory was missing.

Callum saw Hamish drive away before he rang his mother to tell her the news and to ask her to tell Caitlyn. Morag was horrified, but Caitlyn shrugged it off, she believed he'd be back in time for the party. The party, Morag shook, what about the party? What a mess this was!

By the time Saturday arrived, Hamish had heard nothing from the police, despite making a number of phone calls to ask. All he was told, was they were continuing to make enquiries. Hamish was getting more concerned each day, but Isla was frantic, terrified and tearful. Hamish didn't blame her, he felt like crying himself!

Callum was doing a good job running the Estate business, yet all the time; he worried about his friend. Where was Rory? Meanwhile, Caitlyn insisted the party went ahead, convinced Rory would turn up. No one could convince her she'd look foolish if he didn't, that it was best to cancel. Morag was desperate for news of Rory. She had watched him grow up into a pleasant young man. He had spent lots of time with Callum. He had been a constant visitor in her home. She was ashamed of Caitlyn's attitude to Rory's disappearance and knew now Callum was right about the engagement being a mistake, especially on Rory's part. However, she felt trapped by Caitlyn's determination to hold the party and prepared her home and organised the food despite her heart not being in it.

On Saturday night, the first guests arrived from Inverness, all eager to meet Rory. Caitlyn assured them they would soon and loved playing host to her friends. When Hamish and Isla walked in, Morag greeted them close to tears. She admitted Caitlyn had insisted the party go ahead and she couldn't stop her.

"I'm so sorry. Come through to the kitchen," she invited, by now she could easily strangle her daughter. Once she had them settled, she poured coffee and asked if there was any news of Rory. Hamish shook his head, "The police organised a search and so did the Army, but they found nothing. We didn't expect them to of course. We feel Rory is mixed up in something with the Army."

"You must be frantic," Morag whispered, "If I can help, I'm very fond of Rory—Oh, I'm so angry with Caitlyn, I've no idea what to do about this engagement," she stammered.

"Forgive us Morag, but neither are we. It would seem Rory's position is all, Caitlyn is interested in," Isla told her.

"All we want right now is for Rory to come home," Hamish stood up, "Sorry Morag, we can't stay here. This party is—wrong!"

Morag stood too, "I'm so sorry." She followed them out. "Right, I'm going in there and telling everyone the truth," she finally decided and once she had seen Hamish and Isla drive away, she did just that. She began by turning off the music, took a deep breath and began, "I'm sorry to spoil the party, but you are all here under a misunderstanding. Rory is missing, has been missing since Wednesday. The police are searching for him. Caitlyn believed he'd turn up in time for tonight, but as you can see, he hasn't. I'm sure you will all be as concerned as we are. I'm sorry, the party has to end. There is no celebration tonight."

Caitlyn had stood gaping at her mother, "Mum, no," she screamed. One of her friends asked, "Is this true, Cat?"

"Not exactly, he promised to be here," she cried.

"But if he's missing—and where's your ring?" she wondered. "Okay. We're going, your Mum's right, this feels wrong." She gave a contemptuous look at Caitlyn and walked out, followed by half the guests. The rest surrounded Caitlyn, offering sympathy. Caitlyn had never been so embarrassed, ever. Just wait until Rory returned, she'd have something to say about this!

Chapter 6

On the first night in the cellar, Flame insisted Rory slept in the bed. After days incarcerated in the cell, he was exhausted, both physically and mentally. He made no objection which proved her point, she decided, he needed the bed more than she did. She wrapped herself in a blanket and slept on the floor. It was no hardship for a girl who spent nights out in woods and fields, harassing the Germans. She had survived wind, rain and worse in the past. The only trouble was she couldn't sleep. She was fully aware of Rory lying in her bed. His physical presence was deeply affecting her. She had watched him strip and wash just feet from her and her body had re-acted in an alarming way. It took all her willpower to act normally, as he slipped half naked into her bed. Within minutes, he was sound asleep.

Flame stood up and looked closely at him. He was fit, strong and tanned. She guessed he worked out doors a lot of the time, yet his hands were soft, neat with his nails filed. Such hands would sooth an animal, nurse those hurt and stroke a woman, rouse her—. She sighed. How she yearned to touch him, feel him, love him! She drew a deep breath. This had to stop, she had to keep control of herself and the situation she was in, or disaster beckoned them both and her cell mates. Dear God, this was only the first night, there could be many more. She lay back down but sleep was a long time coming.

On Sunday morning, Rory awoke feeling relaxed and refreshed after his first night of proper sleep in days. He sat up slowly as his surroundings brought him back to reality. It all came rushing back. He was trapped in a cellar somewhere in France! A figure moved on the floor and he remembered Flame, the girl who had rescued him from the Germans. He had slept in her bed whilst she slept on the floor. He felt terrible about it, why hadn't he thought last night? He quickly scrambled back into his clothes, dirty, smelly clothes he now discovered. How he wished for just one warm bath and clean underwear!

Flame was awake now as her sixth sense warned her Rory was up. "Morning," she greeted, "I'll make some tea. Later I'll slip out and get some food from friends, who will help us out. I'm sorry, I didn't organise this better, I'm afraid there wasn't enough time. All I can offer you now is black tea and German issue hard biscuits."

"That will do nicely," Rory told her. He was so hungry but would never complain. Memories of breakfasts at home swamped him. Eggs from their chickens, bacon and sausages from the last pig sent to market. His stomach rumbled loudly, and he apologised, "Sorry," he whispered then continued, "Look Flame, about the bed. I shouldn't have taken it last night."

Flame held up her hand, "It's okay Rory, last night you badly needed to rest. Believe me, many a night I'm out having to sleep in worst places than the floor here. Tonight, we'll manage somehow."

"Can you tell me about the things you do?" he asked hesitantly, "Or is it classified information?"

Flame laughed, "I expect it is classified, but I've never signed anything officially secret, whatever. Here's your tea," she also handed over some unappetising biscuits. Rory didn't hesitate, he tucked in gratefully. Flame continued, "Our cell is mainly concerned with supplies, like the ones you brought in and we distribute them. By the way, we found yours and they were badly needed. You did well," she smiled at him and he was pleased. Again, she continued to answer his question, "The airstrip is in our area, so we meet the planes. Sometimes agents come in too, men to work with us, train us, even a woman came one time. Otherwise, we do things to sabotage German activities, anything to delay or stop them."

Rory was listening enthralled. He wanted to hear more. "What about killing?" he whispered.

Flame shook her head. "No, not so far but I would if I had to. I could, we were trained in ways to do so."

"Why do it Flame? I mean, you are young and beautiful. Why risk your life?"

Flame blushed at the compliment but answered instantly, "For France. I am an orphan. I'm alone in the world so there is no one to worry about what I do. Nor is there anyone for me to worry about. I'm free to serve my country."

"You are amazing," Rory told her, and he meant it. She impressed him, attracted him and he knew he already cared about her. He knew he mustn't get involved, he was committed to Caitlyn, yet this woman was ten times better than Caitlyn would ever be. He pulled himself together. Hopefully, he was only here for a few days then he'd be back in the Highlands and his normal life. He did wonder though, if his life could ever be the same after this? However, he had no choice, one day he'd inherit High Tor, he'd employ people who depended on him and he'd never want to let them down and of course, there was Caitlyn.

Flame could see confusion flit across his face and she was curious. What was he thinking? "Tell me about your life back in Scotland," she invited, offering him another hard biscuit.

"Oh, there's not much to tell. I live in the Highlands, running an Estate. There's farms, fishing, hunting and shooting. My parents are alive and live in Inverness."

"Are you married?" she spoke softly and blushed. What was the point in knowing?

"Married, no, but close. Last night, I should have got engaged, we had planned a party," he told her.

A ripple of shock hit Flame, he was engaged! She hid it well and demanded, "Then why, for goodness sake, did you get on that plane?"

Rory shook his head, "I've been trying to work that one out for myself,"

"Is she pretty?" Flame tortured herself by asking. She didn't want to hear he was madly in love with this woman.

"Yes, she is. Her name is Caitlyn and we grew up together in the Highlands. She is eighteen, a brunette with almost black eyes," he grinned, "I'm saying too much, as usual."

"Yes, but only because you love her," Flame sighed.

Rory didn't deny it, and Flame didn't want to hear any more about this Caitlyn! She returned her thoughts to reality, "I'll slip out now and get some food," she decided, "Tomorrow, I'll radio London and let them know you are safe. I have to get to the farm; to my radio. If only I could bring it down here it would be so much easier, but I can't get a signal from here."

"Tell me, how you make contact? Am I right in thinking you are in danger whenever you transmit?" Rory wondered.

"Yes, it's dangerous, the Germans have detectors out and can pinpoint the position we transmit from, hoping to catch us," she admitted. "As for how, we only transmit in code at a pre-arranged time and they reply, giving us new messages." She frowned, "Just lately, I've suspected my code has been broken by a traitor in my cell. It could be why your plane was met by Germans. It's the second time they knew the exact time a plane was due."

"Do you have any idea who he is?" Rory was shocked.

"No, we are only a small group and I'd trust them, but London has warned us it is happening elsewhere too, so it could be anyone. All we can do is continue in hope. One thing I have done is stop anymore drops here for now."

Rory was full of admiration. He exclaimed, "You really are a remarkable woman, Flame."

"No Rory, I am just one of many. We all do our utmost for France. Don't think I'm someone special, because I'm not. I am just one small clog in a secret army of people who love their country." She spoke sharply and Rory remained silent.

Flame fetched her coat and smiled at him, "I'll go now. You must remain hidden here. Do not, under any circumstances leave this cellar. Promise you won't?"

Rory nodded, "Yes, I'll stay here," he agreed and next moment she had gone.

After what seemed like hours, Flame returned. Rory's heart leapt at the sight of her and he admitted silently to himself, this attraction he felt for her wasn't going to be easily dismissed.

Flame brought a number of bags with her. She smiled her delightful smile, unable to hide from herself how attracted she was to Rory. She handed him a bag, "I come bearing gifts. In there are some clean underwear and socks for you. Second hand, I'm afraid and I can't guarantee they'll fit very well, they are the best I could get from a friend."

Rory was touched by her thoughtfulness and thanked her profusely. It was as if she'd read his mind earlier.

From another bag Flame unload bread, cheese, a tin of milk and some tea. Finally, she produced a couple of newspapers. "They should help us pass the time," she told him.

"All this looks like a feast to me after the last few days," Rory was so hungry now, his stomach rumbled at the sight of food, "And as for the clothes, nothing will ever feel as good as those when I put them on."

"All part of the service," Flame smiled happily, "Now, I'm looking forward to a cup of tea with milk." She filled the kettle with water and spread out some bread and cheese.

"Did it go all right, out there? Were there soldiers?" Rory worried.

"It was okay, the soldiers appear to be searching for you still—for us," she added, meaning her cell members. "With luck, London will soon have you out. I'm afraid I can't agree to you flying out from here, it's too dangerous for all of us, with the traitor."

"So, where will I fly from?" Rory suddenly realised he was trapped.

"Who knows, that's for London to arrange. You may not fly, there's always the chance of a boat ride home for you," she laughed.

Horrified, Rory gasped, "How long would that take?" It was all sinking in that he was stuck here, in a cellar for what could be a long time before he got home. It was frightening!

Flame sensed his panic, realising he really had no idea of what he'd got himself involved in. She smiled gently, "Relax Rory. I can't answer your questions. Everything is up to London now. All I can promise you for now is we'll keep you safe whilst you are here."

Rory sighed deeply, "I'm grateful, but that doesn't sound anywhere near to how I feel about you Flame. I owe you everything and I've no idea, how I'll ever repay you."

"I'm pleased to help you. You were brave enough to come here, with our supplies and you will never know how desperate we were for them. You hid them so well the Germans didn't find them, so we are grateful to you too. Anyway, let's eat, you must be starving."

"I am and it looks like a feast. Thank you Flame," Rory helped himself and minutes later they were eating in companionable silence. They then spent the afternoon reading the two newspapers.

"Don't believe all you read," Flame warned him, "They may be in French, but the newspapers are controlled by the Germans."

Despite this Rory devoured the news, page by page, having been deprived of any news for days. He and Flame discussed several articles and he was surprised by her knowledge and intelligence. "Have you studied at University?" he asked her.

Flame burst out laughing, "Me, at University? No Rory, I told you I was an orphan brought up by Nuns," she explained, "At ten, I was adopted out by a school teacher and his wife. They taught me and paid for me to take an accountancy course, when I was old enough."

Rory shook his head, amazed. He compared Flame to Caitlyn, who for all her studies wouldn't have a clue about world events, unlike Flame.

All too soon, night fell once again. Another day to be crossed off Rory realised. Tomorrow was Monday, nearly a week since he left Scotland. How were his parents coping? Had someone rescued Bonny in time? How long ago it all seemed to him. Tonight, Flame went and fetched a blanket from the chest. She was embarrassed he could see, as he watched her roll it up into a long strip and place it down the centre of the bed. "You one side, me the other, that way we can share the bed," she announced huskily.

Rory stared at her, "Is that wise? I mean, you don't really know me, do you? Let me sleep on the floor." He was floundering, embarrassed at the excitement the mere thought of sharing a bed with her brought!

"I'll take my chances," Flame turned away, knowing he was correct, she wanted him, it was as simple as that, yet even now she realised the danger she was putting herself in. She turned away to wash. When she'd finished, Rory did the same before getting in to one side of the bed. Flame blew out the candle before getting in the other side.

Rory tried to lay motionless, for he knew just one touch, accidental or not, would break his resolve to behave as a gentleman should. Yet, his body was in agony for her, and he considered leaving the bed.

Flame too was having trouble. She was so aware of Rory's body next to her, but in contrast to Rory, she was revelling in the sensations his body aroused. She was playing with fire. She knew

43

but couldn't stop herself. She was totally captivated by him. He was ruggedly attractive, he was strong, yet he was a gentleman too. She somehow knew he'd been raised with morals and good manners and he'd never take advantage of her. What a fool she was, he could be gone in days and she'd never see him again. She breathed in the scent of him, admittedly he needed a bath, she grinned, but he was male, all male and her senses soared. No one had ever stirred her up like this before. She tried to relax.

Rory wasn't sleeping either, she could tell. Was he aware of her, she wondered? Did his body respond to hers? "Rory," she whispered huskily.

"Yes!" he was instantly on alert and turned towards her. His arm fell across her and his hand tangled in her hair." Flame—no!" he groaned, but it was too late. His hands cupped her face as her body met his, the blanket tossed aside. Rory needed no invitation after that. His hand snaked around her neck, pulling her face to his and their lips met. Hungrily they devoured each other, until frustrated by their clothes they began removing them. Finally naked, all reason gone, Rory groped for sanity, "Flame, are you sure about this?" He had to know, had to make just one attempt to let her stop, if she wanted to. "I'm sure," she whispered, "No regrets."

"None," he admitted, hoping he'd still mean it tomorrow! He moved over her, needing her desperately, pulling her closer and closer, his hands and his lips exploring her, her hands arousing him even further, until they were both gasping.

Rory was bold, demanding yet gentle with her, wanting to give her pleasure as well as accepting it from her. Flame returned each kiss, each touch with even more excitement as she offered herself in sheer abandonment. When Rory took her, it was like neither of them had experience such joy before. Afterwards they fell into an exhausted sleep, locked in each other's arms, only to wake before dawn broke to repeat the whole performance with equal satisfaction to them both.

Chapter 7

On Monday morning, Inspector Harris turned up early at the McGregor's home in Inverness. Hamish invited him into their sitting room and called Isla. Good news or bad, it was best she heard it from the Inspector, he decided. When they were all sitting down the Inspector began, "I have some news for you Mr McGregor, but rather frustrating news I'm afraid. It would appear your son Rory, is at present helping the Army. I'm told you have no need to concern yourselves—please," he stopped as Isla exploded.

"No need for concern!" she cried, "we have no idea where Rory is, tell me how we cannot be concerned."

"I do understand Mrs McGregor, but the more questions I ask, the less I'm told. I cannot tell you, where Rory is or what he's doing. I don't know if he's well or whether he wants to be where he is. I don't know if he's in danger or not. I'm so sorry, but I've been told to back off. You must appreciate the Army have the upper hand in this. They simply close up and quote all information is top secret"

"Did they give you any idea when he'd return home?" Hamish asked.

"No, they didn't. I can only repeat how sorry I am to have not found out more," Inspector Harris sighed, "I'm far from happy about this secrecy myself."

Hamish nodded, "The Army at High Tor are training secret agents, I believe. Which leads me to think Rory might be in France," he mused. "If he is, he's had no training for whatever he's doing. He has to be in great danger."

Isla cried out and Hamish put an arm about her before continuing, "It's best we now face facts, love. We cannot ignore the possibilities any longer."

"I have no reason to confirm your fears, Mr McGregor, but if truth be told, I came to think along those lines myself. I repeat, I have no information to support your theory." Inspector Harris stood up, "I can see nothing else we can do for now, except wait."

"What for, to hear Rory's been killed in France?" Isla demanded angrily, "Will they even tell us that, if it happens?"

For a moment, Inspector Harris looked uncertain, "I would think they'd have to," he mumbled.

Tears filled Isla's eyes and trickled down her face. "So, we may never know," she whispered, and the pain tore at Hamish's heart.

"I'm sure, if we're patient Rory will turn up one day," the Inspector tried to ease the situation.

Hamish stood up too. "Thank you for coming and for doing your best for us. If you do hear any more—please," he couldn't say more.

"Of course, I will Mr McGregor. That goes without saying," he moved towards the door and they shook hands. Hamish saw him out.

Hamish was angry, so angry, and he knew he couldn't simply wait as the Inspector had suggested. This was his son, everyone seemed to be dismissing so casually. Well, someone was going to find out he wasn't going to sit back and accept the situation easily. He needed answers, now!

Isla was in the kitchen, weeping silently. His heart went out to her. "How about you make us some coffee, love, then I'll tell you what I've decided to do."

Isla nodded and blew her nose. She put the kettle on before turning to Hamish, "I'm so worried, Rory's been missing for days now."

"I know and we're no further forward. That's why I've decided to go to High Tor and confront the General," Hamish told her. "He needs to know, we aren't people he can dismiss like this. We are desperate for answers."

Isla looked calmer, he was pleased to see; however, she frowned again, "Callum said, he'd gone to London," she reminded him.

"Yes, I remember, but hopefully he'll be back by now. If he's not, there must be someone else in charge up there, I'll see them. I've got to do something."

"I know. I keep seeing Rory hurt somewhere, lost and afraid, desperate to come home," Isla shed more tears.

"Well stop imagining. Let's wait until we know what we're dealing with," Hamish told her firmly. "Anyway, we could be wrong. Rory could be having the time of his life!" he smiled. He didn't believe a word of it.

"Shall I come with you to see the General?" Isla wondered.

"No, I may have more chance of getting in the House if I'm alone. Don't worry if I'm late home, I intend to stay there long enough to get answers. I'll ring you from the Stables immediately, if I've any news," he promised.

"I'll pray you are successful. Not knowing where Rory is has to be the worst experience of my life," Isla told him. Hamish hugged her and kissed her goodbye. As if he didn't feel exactly the same.

When Hamish arrived at High Tor, he went first to see Callum in the Stables office. Callum jumped up, "Is there any news?" he asked anxiously.

"Nothing definite I'm afraid, or I'd have rung you. The Inspector told us this morning that Rory's disappearance is connected to the Army."

"I knew the General lied to me that morning. What happens now?" Callum wondered.

"Nothing as far as they are concerned, but that's why I'm here. I'm going to confront the General. Do you know if he's back from London?" Hamish asked.

"I've not seen him but that doesn't mean anything. They all seem to hide away over there," Callum told him. "What I find hard to believe is Rory even getting involved with that lot."

"I agree with you. Does that mean he's been forced into something?"

Callum shook his head, worried, "I don't know."

"Nor do I," Hamish sighed, "Right, I'm going to see the General, get some answers. I'll report back," he stood up to leave.

"I wish you luck, I do hope you find out," Callum watched him go.

Security was tight as Hamish approached the House. On being challenged, he asked quietly to see the General. He gave his name and pointed out that this was still his home officially.

That surprised the soldier who showed him into a small room just off the entrance hall. It was Hamish's old study, obviously now used as a waiting room. One soldier disappeared; whilst another stood guard outside the door.

Hamish waited and waited. All around him was silence, no movements, no people except the one guard. It was unnerving, but he determined to stick it out. Finally, he heard footsteps and in strode the General.

"Mr McGregor, I'm sorry to keep you waiting," he offered to shake hands. Hamish gave a cursory shake.

Hamish went straight on the attack, "I'll not take up your time, General. You can guess, why I'm here. My son Rory is missing and I've been told you know his whereabouts."

"Really McGregor, you know I cannot reveal classified information," the General spoke smoothly. He had obviously prepared his answers before coming down.

"I'm not asking you to reveal secrets, but I do want to know where my son is and to be re-assured he is alive and well," Hamish spoke sharply, "Oh and when he'll be home."

"I cannot answer your questions. I can only assure you the situation your son is in, he made of his own free will," the General replied.

"Is he well?" Hamish continued to push.

"He is, to my knowledge."

"Is he in danger?" whispered Hamish.

"I cannot say. I'm sorry, Mr McGregor I must go. I'm not long back from London and I've a pile of work waiting," the General hesitated, "I'm sure you are worried about your son and I wish I could help. I've got to know him over past months and found him a pleasant young man. If any information comes to light, that I can share with you, I will," he promised then regretted it. He had no hope of keeping it.

Hamish knew he would hear nothing more and stood up. "Then, I'll not keep you any longer. Good day General," he strode out.

The General watched him go, grateful the interview was over. If only Hamish knew the can of worms Rory had opened by getting on that plane! He himself had been summoned to London like a naughty schoolboy, questioned none stop and reprimanded over everything from using Rory as a driver, to exposing him to classified information. He had tried to explain the terrain out here and how useless military drivers were out on the moors, but no one listened to him. As for Rory, all they knew was the pilot's report, (and he'd been severely reprimanded for taking Rory). The General would be surprised, if Rory got out of France alive. London was waiting on a radio transmission, later today for any news of Rory. If it was bad news; he hoped it wouldn't be him given the job of telling Hamish.

Chapter 8

On Monday morning, Rory woke feeling warm and satiated by their night of love making. He felt wonderful. Flame still slept, his arm close around her, her body curled into his. He marvelled at her small form, yet she had been so passionate last night, her staying power equal to his. She had been generous in giving him the most exquisite pleasure and that spoke volumes. They had made love, not just had sex. He was totally in love with her, he knew that without doubt. Did she feel the same? He stretched lazily, the movement waking her. For a moment her eyes embraced him, shining with happiness. Rory pulled her even closer, raining kisses on her face and her eyes. His lips covered hers tenderly, softly and Flame responded briefly before pulling away.

"Rory, we mustn't!" she gasped, "We should never have started this. I'm to blame."

Rory was hurt, stunned by her rejection. "Why not, what blame?" he demanded.

"Because we've made a mistake," she tried to sit up, pull away from him but Rory forced her back onto the bed and towered over her. "You can't tell me last night was a mistake!" he growled, "You made love to me with feelings so deep, it was wonderful. I loved you too and I know I'll never feel that with anyone else. How can you deny it?"

Flame's eyes filled with tears, "I can't, we did make love, I feel love for you, but for goodness sake Rory, look where we are. We're in the middle of fighting a deadly war. Our feelings can mean nothing. Love cannot last here, we will never be together, never see each other again. What we had last night was a brief, wonderful night together, but it ends here."

Rory was shocked. No way, could he simply dismiss last night as the end. She had to be wrong. He was still holding her down. His mouth came down on hers and he teased her with butterfly kisses. Flame moaned softly as his lips caressed her throat and moved down to her breasts. "Rory," she whispered huskily. His hands were tormenting her body,

"Oh Flame, I love you," he insisted.

"I love you, Rory," she cried surrendering to him, opening to him, her hands rousing him even higher. Their love making was even greater than the night before.

They awoke again later that morning. This time Flame got out of bed and made some tea. She had to get to the farm in time for her radio slot. For a brief moment, she stared down at Rory who was still sleeping. Oh, he was gorgeous, wonderful and he loved her. She couldn't deny her feeling for him either but oh, what a fix they were in and how foolish she had been to instigate this. When it was time for her to leave; she woke Rory with a cup of tea.

Rory jumped, instantly awake and she gave him a gentle kiss, "Sorry to wake you but it's time for me to go—time for my radio slot. There's food left so help yourself and I'll bring more back later. Please stay here and don't worry, I will be back."

"You should have woken me earlier. Please be careful, I do love you," he kissed her again before she left.

Flame arrived at the farm with time to spare before her transmission. She went in search of Yves and found him in a barn with a cow in labour. Yves was married with two children but with the invasion of France imminent, he had sent his wife and children to her parents in England. He had joined the Resistance and met Flame and offered her the flat above his barn.

Yves greeted Flame warmly and Flame moved nearer the cow, "Is she having trouble?" she wanted to know.

"Yes, it's taking too long but I think things are moving now. How is our guest?"

"Doing well, I'm having a break and picking up some food," she told him. She never told a soul, when a radio broadcast was due. At that moment, the cow gave a loud bellow and Yves turned back to it. "Oh yes, I see a hoof!" he exclaimed. Flame watched amazed as he grabbed a rope and knotted it around two tiny feet.

"Next contraction, I can help by pulling," he explained.

Flame watched closely as Yves began pulling, not a light tug but heavy efforts that had Flame cringing for the poor cow. Next moment, she too grabbed the rope to help and out slid a young calf, falling into the straw. Yves rubbed it hard with hay and next moment it was breathing well.

"She was too big, but she'll do now," he grinned at Flame, before dragging the calf forward to its Mum's head. The cow immediately began licking it and Flame watched mesmerized by the whole scene.

"I've never seen anything so amazing," she admitted.

"Yes, it is special," Yves admitted, "Like a cup of tea?" he offered, washing his hands in a bucket of water.

"I'd love one, but I need to get back to our guest. I just need some things from the flat. I'll see you soon Yves," she waved goodbye.

In her little flat, Flame had time for a change of clothes before setting out her code books and preparing her message. At the last minute, she got her radio out of its hiding place and switched it on. She tapped in her call sign and followed it with the message.

In London, two men waited impatiently for the operator to write down Flame's message. He quickly decoded it and handed it to one of the men. The two men exclaimed in unison,

"He's safe, thanks be!" One of them handed the operator the reply, already in code, "Send this back, please."

Waiting in France, Flame heard her call sign and wrote out the message, before signing off. She hid the radio before settling to decode the message. She read it in surprise, "Move parcel 55 (obviously Rory) to cell 25 by Wednesday, p.m., for return." Rory was going home! She would never see him again! Her heart was breaking, she loved him so much. Never in her life had she been so overwhelmed by a man. Now she had to watch him go, any future for them was impossible, hadn't she told him so this morning? For the first time in her life she had found someone who loved her, and it wasn't to be. If life had treated her badly so far, now it was being downright cruel.

Rory was going home, she repeated, London had arranged it and her orders were clear. She had to move him to cell 25, so she better get on and do it! She had heard about cell 25 but never met any of them, to her knowledge. They were a wild bunch who lived in caves and were killers by reputation. The leader she'd heard was a huge giant of a man, code named Bear and he ruled with a rod of iron. There was even a rumour; he'd killed one of his own men for challenging his leadership. Flame shuddered, and she had to hand Rory over to them. She got out some maps and planned a route. At least, she had time on her side for cell 25 was only twenty-five to thirty miles from Villenue. She would have to avoid main roads and use countryside, wherever possible. Getting out of Villenue was the most dangerous part, due to sentries posted at exits. Finally, she was satisfied with her chosen route and memorized each stage. She would never carry documents or maps in case she was stopped and searched.

Flame had one final fear. For the past few weeks, she'd worried about her code being broken. Was there any chance this message to move Rory was a trap? There was no way she could find out and getting Rory home safely had to be her priority. This was a risk she had to take.

Flame collected up all the papers, maps and documents and hid everything away safely before leaving the flat. She slipped away from the farm without seeing Yves and began the walk back into town. She bought more food and hurried back to the cellar all the while aware she and Rory had just one more night together before they set out for cell 25. She had already decided they had to leave Villenue on Tuesday, in daylight and camp out Tuesday night to arrive by Wednesday lunchtime.

Rory stared at her in disbelief. "You are handing me over to someone else? Why, because we slept together? Oh Flame, don't do this, I love you, I can't leave you."

"Of course, you have to leave, don't be naive Rory. You aren't listening to me, are you? This move has nothing to do with us. This is orders from London. I have no say in the matter. They want you back, badly it seems, and they have arranged this move."

Rory stepped forward, preparing to take her in his arms, but she pushed him away, "No, don't, this is going to be hard on both of us." Again, Rory moved forward forcing her into his arms.

"Flame, please don't." His lips joined with hers and she was lost. She melted into his arms, her hands curling around his neck and she returned his kisses with passion. However, once again she broke free.

53

"Everything is against us Rory, you shouldn't even be here. We should never have met."

"We were meant to meet, fate decreed it and one day, I know fate will grant us a life together, nothing will stop us," Rory insisted.

"Please face reality just once, Rory. You have a fiancée waiting for you and a business to run. Before long, you won't even remember me. There can be no happy endings for us," Flame was close to tears. She knew she'd never forget him.

"I will never forget you Flame, believe me, my love."

"I do want to, oh I do," this time Flame surrendered herself into his arms and next moment Rory swept her up into his arms and onto the bed.

"We still have tonight," he whispered, as his kisses claimed hers. They stayed awake long into the night making love. Occasionally, Flame felt tears wet on her face knowing this was all she would ever have with Rory and her heart was breaking. They had had three nights together, here in the cellar and two of those nights had been spent in each other's arms. It was a cruel fate that was parting them so soon, but what choice did Flame have? Rory had to leave.

Flame awoke first. She was laid entwined with Rory's body, his arm tight around her, one hand cupping her breast. He was in a deep sleep and Flame hated waking him. This was it, the finale, she had no choice. She kissed him as she moved slowly to disentangle herself from him. He stirred slowly finally waking his eyes meeting hers. He knew this was it. Flame heated water and made tea. "We need to eat and get away from here. Once we're in the countryside, it will get easier," she assured him.

"How far do we have to go?" he wondered. He had finally accepted he had no choice.

"About thirty miles roughly," she told him as she began packing a bottle of water and a torch in a bag. "Come and eat," she invited, "then we'll take what's left with us."

Rory had dressed meantime. He accepted some bread and ham and sat down to eat; whilst Flame made more tea. She added the rest of the bread to her bag and fetched a blanket off the bed. She folded this up to take too.

"I'll never forget this place," Rory whispered. Flame couldn't speak for a moment, it all felt raw this morning. "Right, we must go, I want to be out of Villenue as soon as possible. Stay close to me Rory and if we're stopped, let me do the talking." She hesitated, "Pray, we aren't stopped," she added.

Today was Tuesday, just one week since he'd got on the plane that night. One week that had felt like a lifetime, a week that had changed his life forever, for he knew he'd never be the same man, he'd been before.

As he stepped out of the cellar the cold bright day greeted him and he gulped in fresh air after days underground. It felt so good, he'd never take sunshine and fresh air for granted again, he swore.

"Let's get a move on," Flame insisted, as she led the way and Rory followed closely. Flame was once again a Resistance leader, at war with the enemy and all her senses were on high alert.

The journey was fraught with danger. There were soldiers everywhere, stopping people at random, demanding passes and ID's. Flame was experienced enough to think ahead. She weaved this way and that, avoiding known check points and sticking with groups of people so as not to be out in the open and obvious. By late afternoon, they were finally out of Villenue and ahead Rory could see fields and woods. He relaxed slightly, keeping close to Flame.

Flame was thrilled to make it out of Villenue. No one knew better than her how dangerous the past few hours had been. However, she never showed any emotion, never confided in Rory; how scared she had been at times. She was once again wholly Resistance, attempting to complete her task successfully.

They had made good time as darkness fell. The evening grew colder and Flame felt able to safely call a halt. Travelling at night brought its own problems, like falling on rough ground or walking blind into a German trap. She searched for a barn or outbuilding to take cover in and finally one came into view. It lay some distance from the farm house. She scanned the area for farm dogs but couldn't see any. It was ideal and in no time, they were up the ladder into a hay loft. There was even some straw covering the floor and this with the blanket they soon had a comfortable bed, for the night. They ate the bread and drank the water and lay down close to one another.

Dawn found them stiff but well refreshed by sleep and they quickly set off again. They reached the caves soon after noon. The area around them was rough and wild, strewn with rocks and boulders. Flame approached cautiously, settling down close to the ground and Rory automatically followed her lead. Flame knew this was the time of reckoning, if the traitor knew they were here if this was a trap! She considered her options. She could walk in alone and be caught. They could walk in together and be caught. Or it could all be okay, the message genuine and Rory on his way home. She had to decide and had turned to Rory when suddenly a movement behind her had her spinning round terrified. She had made a huge mistake. Two men stood there, their rifles pointed straight at them both.

Chapter 9

The plane circled around and began dropping down to earth. Outside, it was pitch black and Rory had no idea where they were. He no longer cared. Everything had happened so fast. He had immediately been separated from Flame; the moment the two men had appeared, and he never saw her again. There had been no chance to even say goodbye. Now, he was arriving 'somewhere in England' according to the pilot. Not Scotland. It was only a tiny plane, smaller than the one he'd travelled in to France. There was just one other man on board who didn't speak to him and the pilot. The plane landed smoothly and came to a gentle stop. He was home again yet felt nothing. The door swung open and a soldier stood there. "McGregor, follow me sir," he ordered, and Rory did as he was told. The second man simply disappeared into the darkness.

A large building loamed out of the gloom and Rory realised it was a grand looking house. They passed a sentry at the door and went inside. The light nearly blinded Rory. He had travelled in darkness for hours. An officer greeted him,

"Mr McGregor, welcome home. We'll find you some food and a bed for tonight and talk tomorrow."

"Talk-tomorrow, can't I go home now?" Rory questioned wearily.

"You will have to be de-briefed first. Come this way," he was told.

Rory was shown upstairs and into an en suite room. His eyes immediately settled on the shower and toilet. Oh, what bliss!

"You will be brought up some food shortly. There are clean clothes in the wardrobe and soap and things in the bathroom. Tomorrow, you will be shown the way downstairs. Goodnight." As he left; Rory thought he heard a click. Had they locked him in? By now, he was past caring. He stripped everything off, fully aware at how disgusting his clothes smelt. He then stood under the shower for an extremely long time, the pure joy of hot water and soap unimaginable. Finally, feeling clean at last he wrapped himself in a soft towel and waited. The pleasure soon continued when a tap on his door announced a soldier with a tray heaped with food. Rory savoured every mouthful, ate every last morsel, had food ever tasted so good, he wondered? By then, he was exhausted and fell into a beautiful soft clean bed, to sleep the deepest of sleeps.

Rory was woken next morning and taken down to the mess room, where he was served a full English breakfast. However, he was instantly aware that he was being kept apart from the other men present. He was also 'guarded' by the soldier who had fetched him. He had little to say.

All too soon he was told, 'They' were ready for him and he was taken to a small interview room where the questions began and lasted for three days. Why had he got on the plane? Who had met him in France? Where had the Germans taken him? Had they tortured him? Who had rescued him, and how? Where had they hidden him? Who had moved him to get the plane home? How had they got him out of Villenue? Each time the answer came up as Flame, they wanted to know who Flame was. When he told them a woman, it had aroused a great deal of interest. How old was she? What did she look like? How had she treated him? It was obvious to Rory that they had no idea a woman ran the cell out there. The questions were endless, and Rory tried hard to keep his temper as the same questions were repeated over and over. He answered everything truthfully, told them everything he knew, all that had happened to him—except the nights of passion he'd shared with Flame. Those, he considered were his secret to keep!

Each time Flame's name came up, or he recounted an incident involving her, pain filled him. He couldn't bear the pain parting from her was causing him. The worry over what had happened to her after he left, kept him awake at night. He did ask what had happened to the agent who had been taken ill at the plane that night and was told he had suffered a burst appendix. He was still recovering in hospital. As for the pilot who had taken him to France, he'd been severely reprimanded. He'd known it wrong to take an untrained civilian out to France.

On the fourth morning there, Rory was awake early for some reason and thinking clearly at last. He wanted to go home, he decided, it was as simple as that. Today, he would insist on being released. He had only a vague idea of military law, but surely it didn't apply to him, a civilian? Surely, they couldn't keep him here? He was feeling like a prisoner all over again. Okay, he was in a very nice prison, comfortable room, good food, but all the time shadowed by a guard, who kept him separate from anyone else. He wanted to go home.

After breakfast, he was once again escorted to the interview room. He breathed deeply, he was ready!

"Good morning," Rory took the initiative, "I wish to request you release me, let me go home. I have told you everything I know, everything I can. I have co-operated to the best of my ability. I have nothing left to tell. May I remind you, I am only a civilian after all," he stopped to draw breath.

One of the officers shouted angrily, "A civilian who involved himself in a military operation, without permission or thought. You got yourself into a dangerous situation from which we had to rescue you! Do you know how many people's lives you endangered from your thoughtless actions?" He paused then continued, "Mr McGregor, I could right now sign a document for your imprisonment until the end of the war. You are in possession of top secret information. You may be a civilian, but we are working under war time rules. Do you understand?"

Rory sat in his chair, silenced. Was the officer speaking the truth? Could they imprison him? He changed tack, "Look I apologise. I have said how grateful I am to you, for rescuing me. I made a mistake, but that poor man was insisting on going when he was incapable of doing so. I simply took his place."

The second officer took over, "Mr McGregor, look at it from our point of view. You are in possession of information which is classified top secret. You know far too much for us to let you go. You must see that?"

Rory's heart sank, he could see the sense in what they were saying, but he wasn't about to capitulate that easily.

"I live in the Highlands of Scotland, so I am hardly likely to meet anyone interested in what I know. I am needed at home, I have a large estate to run—and," he was rudely interrupted.

"Then, it's a pity you didn't consider that before you flew off to France!"

"I have apologised so many times," Rory sighed wearily, this was exhausting, and he wondered how much longer he could endure it. He tried again, "I have asked before about my parents and girlfriend. Do they know I'm here?"

"Of course, they don't!" the man exploded, amazed Rory could even consider such a thing possible.

"They have been told you are safe," the second man told Rory. "You have put them through a very worrying time."

Rory believed that, and he was beaten. He was truly sorry when he thought of his parents and what he'd put them through.

"We'll stop now. I don't see continuing this today," the officer turned to Rory. "You can rest in your room." Rory stood up. For the first time here, he felt helpless and alone. He could see no end to this. His guard appeared and led him back upstairs. Rory heard the click again as his door was locked.

Flame was back in Villenue, having made the return journey the day following Rory's departure. The two men with rifles had led her and Rory into the caves; where they met the cell leader, Bear. Rory was immediately removed, and Flame never saw him again. Flame recognised Bear from the rumours she'd heard about him. He was a giant of a man, dressed in rough worn clothes. He had told her that Rory was being removed to the airstrip, ready for that night.

"Who would you be?" Bear asked Flame.

"I'm Flame," she finally found her voice, totally overawed by this man. His eyebrows rose in surprise. "You are Flame. No one told me you were a woman!" he actually laughed. "I've heard about you. Is it true you have an infiltrator in your cell?"

Flame could see no reason to deny it, so she nodded, still a little wary.

"Have you any idea who he is?" Bear pushed, and Flame finally found her voice, "Only a possible lead. We are a small cell and I can't eliminate anyone yet"

"There have been problems in other cells too. You need to be careful, Flame," he told her gently. "Come and have something to eat. By the way, a package arrived for you from London. It's a new code system and change of radio frequency."

Flame stifled a protest. He'd been through the package meant for her! She was cross but hid it. "Thanks, that could help," she nodded as he led her deeper into the cave.

"When you've eaten, I'll find you somewhere to sleep tonight."

Bear saw the flicker of fear in her eyes and smiled gently, "Don't worry Flame. You will be under my protection and no one would dare to go near you, whilst you're with me!"

In the end, Flame ate and slept well that night and left early the following morning. In the middle of the night, she woke to the throb of a plane's engine, flying close overhead. Tears filled her eyes and she whispered, "Goodbye my love," and cried herself silently back to sleep. The next morning, Bear told her happily, "Your package made a seamless get-a-way last night. It went like clockwork."

When Bear wished her goodbye, he sent two men to escort her for a while. It wasn't necessary as far as she was concerned, but Flame was experience enough to know Bear wanted her well clear of his patch, in the unlikely event of her being caught by the Germans.

Back in the cellar, Flame mourned Rory for two days. His presence was here. She felt him and yearned for him. At night, she cried for him and all day she sat remembering their time together here. On the third day, she woke up and made the decision, no more. She would move back to the farm and take up her Resistance duties again. The first problem to solve was who the traitor was, so she could re-instate drops. Rory was gone; she finally accepted, and she would never see him again, she needed to get on with her life.

Back at the farm, Yves greeted her warmly, "I wondered, when I'd see you again."

"I've been busy getting our guest away," she told him.

His face showed shock, "Not from here, I trust?"

"No, he went further afield. Now, he's gone I can concentrate on our own problems. Still good to know we did a difficult rescue, well. I'll be at the flat for a while," she advised him.

Alone in the flat, Flame took out the package given to her by Bear and studied it. She took out her radio from its hiding place and re-tuned it to the new frequency. She sent out a test call to

London, giving her call sign and closed down. London would now know she had received the package and was available on the new frequency. She now turned her attention to the new code system. It was different to the old one, but she could see no problems with it. Her next thoughts were whether it was now safe to resume drops. Was there a traitor or had the Germans simply broken her code when listening in? If so, she was in danger, as they could know her location. This meant she would have to move, just in case, she decided sadly. This flat had been ideal. The obvious place to move to was the cellar, but she couldn't transmit from there. However, for her own safety she would move her radio down there today, she decided. As for more drops, before her next radio contact with London, she would ask her cell mates for their thoughts. For herself, she couldn't wait. Her sole purpose in belonging to the Resistance was actually organising the drops of essential supplies.

Her thoughts then turned to the second problem. Was there a traitor in her cell? The evidence did point to it. She quickly ran through her members. Yves she knew well. She trusted him as she did Gervaise, who was married with children. There was also the 'Forger' as he was known, but she knew very little about him and as he worked for other cells too, well, she had put him on top of the lists of suspects. There were also Tom and Huw, Welsh brothers who ran a vine-yard outside Villenue. They had left it too late to escape back to England and been trapped once the Germans invaded France. They were young and keen and had been reliable so far. Flame didn't want to suspect them. She had no idea who it was, she sighed. If there was a traitor, she could only hope he'd give himself away one day, so she could kill him! She hadn't killed so far, but she'd do it, she swore.

Chapter 10

Rory McGregor was causing headaches for the powers that be. The General from High Tor was once again summoned to London. The situation was unique. A civilian, a VIP no less, had unbelievably been transported into France, met up with the Germans and the Resistance and put numerous people in danger, on both sides of the channel to get him back. Now he was back, in possession of top secret information, what did they do with him? He himself had raised a point of law too, how far did military law apply to civilians? Letting him go, some said was putting people's lives at risk, but could they keep him somewhere secure, legally?

The General had been held responsible for all this mess, from the beginning and he was now asked to find a solution. From the first time he had met Rory, he had liked the young man. He had seen him as hard working and sincere. He alone had not been surprised to hear Rory had taken his agents place on the plane. If only he had returned the same night, no one would ever have known. He'd have torn Rory off a strip and hushed it up. No one had been more worried when he hadn't returned, except of course, Rory's family. Now here he was, back in London and been given the chance to have Rory released. He hesitated, played for time. He delayed making his decision for pure effect. He couldn't race in with his wish to take Rory home!

He called a meeting. "This is a catch twenty-two situation, if ever there was one," he began, "I am fully aware of the risks of letting McGregor go. I am also concerned about the McGregor family. If we can't tell them something concrete soon, I fear they will be taking matters to the top. Don't forget who they are, they are well connected to some high-ranking officials." Again, he paused for effect. "There is also the need for McGregor to return home. His estate is classed as 'essential' to the war effort. It provides vast amounts of food to the Agricultural Ministry, but without his expertise and overseeing the operation, I can see it failing. He was refused permission to join the forces because of it." He paused for breath, looking to see if his words were swaying his audience. It was impossible to say. "Summing up, I believe we should return him home. The Highlands are a lonely place, I should know. Not many people live there and as I'm actually living there at present, I would take responsibility for him. He has already signed the official secrets act, so that's covered. As I was the one who allowed him to drive for us, it's the least I can do."

Some of the officers present continued to insist Rory knew too much to be set free, but as they had no other solution, the decision was made. Rory was to be released into the General's care and everyone sighed with relief. A difficult situation had been resolved.

Rory was summoned and in front of a number of high ranking officers, was told he was being allowed home, under the General's eye. He was given a list of conditions to which he willingly agreed. He just wanted to go home and next moment he was handed over to the General. He grasped his hand gratefully.

"I'm so glad to see you, General," he told him.

"Not as glad as I am, to see you. Have you any idea of the trouble you've caused everyone? Never mind, let's get you out of here. You can stay at my hotel tonight. Tomorrow, we must have a serious talk before we set off home."

Rory nodded. "I can't wait to go home," he sighed. "By the way, where are we?"

"Somewhere in Surrey, we'll go by train tomorrow. Come on, I could do with a drink right now and I doubt you'll say no to a glass of whisky." Just like Rory, he couldn't wait to get back to High Tor. He had had more than enough of London to last him a lifetime.

The following morning, Rory was called early to the General's room in the hotel. They sat down, and the General began, "Before we leave for home, I need to make sure you are fully aware of the conditions under which you have been released."

"Yes, I am unable to tell anyone where I've been or who I met," Rory nodded. "Or leave High Tor."

"Not talking about what happen to you won't be that simple. Not when your dad pushes you for answers, which he will. You have put both your parents through torture, Rory. They have involved the Army and the police trying to find you."

Rory turned pale, he hadn't thought about that. "I'm sorry."

"I hope you are. So, many people were affected by your actions. Right as I said, you must not tell anyone anything. If you do, it's me who has to report you. When we get home, I'll have a chat to your parents, try and explain."

Rory nodded again, trying to take all this in. "When will we be home?" he asked. It was all he thought about. Today was Sunday.

"We should get there sometime tomorrow. We'll get the nine o'clock train today, if it even runs. The war time timetables are impossible to work out. We'll stay the night in Edinburgh when we get there and get a car to take us to High Tor, the next day. This morning, I sent a telegram to your dad, saying we hoped to be home Monday."

Rory thanked him, "I should have thought of that," he admitted.

"It is going to take you a long time to get back to normal, if you ever do. I have read your reports on France, but did you tell London everything? I need to know if there's anything else for me to deal with, if so, best you tell me now."

For a moment Rory hesitated, and the General noticed, but then Rory shook his head, "No, I'm sure I covered everything."

"Well, we'll be having plenty of time to talk once we're home. Please confide in me, don't bottle it all up. Especially, when you are questioned by people and can't tell them what happened," the General told him.

"Thanks, General, I will," Rory agreed, "I am grateful for your help and I won't forget what you've done for me."

"That's okay lad," the General smiled.

Monday afternoon, the limousine pulled into the stable yard at High Tor. Waiting impatiently were Hamish, Isla and Callum. However, the first person to reach Rory was Bonny. She literally threw herself at him, barking in ecstasy and smothering him in fur and licks. Rory fell to his knees with her and hugged her, his face awash with tears.

Callum was next but stood to one side as Isla grasped her son in her arms. She was in floods of tears. "Oh Rory, Rory, where have you been, we've been out of our minds with worry."

Hamish refused to wait and he too, pushed in and took Rory in a bear hug, "Oh son, oh it's good to have you back."

Rory disentangled himself, keeping a hold on both of his parents. "Oh, I'm so sorry, so sorry," he gasped, still tearful.

Callum now stepped forward, "Good to have you back Rory. You did have us worried," he admitted giving him a hug.

"I didn't mean to, I'm so sorry," Rory repeated overwhelmed.

"Shall we go inside? I have something to say to you all," the General took over and they all trooped up to the office. Once inside, he simply told them quite clearly that Rory was only here because he was sworn to secrecy about where he'd been. "I am asking you all not to question him. If he gives away any information, he is at risk of being removed from here until the end of the war. Also, Rory must remain here on High Tor, not leave the area."

"But we are his parents—we are entitled to know where he's been," Isla objected.

"No, I'm afraid you aren't," the General told her firmly, "Rory is unable to tell you anything. Please, just be happy he's home again and give him time to adjust to life here."

"I'm sure, we are grateful to you," Hamish said, "and we will abide by your wishes. We are just so happy to have him home."

"Yes, yes, of course and we thank you for bringing him home," Isla added. Callum remained silent, watching closely. He was shocked by Rory's obvious distress. He was sitting in his chair with his hands on Bonny's head, clinging to her. He was confused, it seemed. Where had he been and what had happened to him, Callum wondered, afraid for his friend.

The General was leaving, and Isla and Hamish were thanking him again. He turned to Rory, "I'll be over tomorrow morning," he told him. He disappeared down the stairs.

Callum decided it was best if he left Rory with his parents for a while. He gripped Rory's shoulder, "I'll just go over and tell Mum, the good news that you are home. She'll be thrilled. I'll pop back later for a chat, shall I?"

Rory looked up and nodded, "I'd like that Callum." Pleased Callum nodded to Hamish and left.

Once alone with his parents, Rory sat up and faced them. "I'm so sorry. I can't imagine what I've put you through. I wish I hadn't –wish I'd thought first," he shuddered.

"What did you do?" Hamish whispered, "Oh, I know we shouldn't ask, but look at you son—you're in such a state."

"I wish I could say, but you know I can't. I've caused so much trouble and I'm sorry." Rory stammered. "If I talk, they will send me to prison."

Isla had watched horrified, "No oh no, I can't believe that."

Hamish asked, "Were you forced into whatever it was?"

"No, I volunteered Dad. In some ways, I'm not sorry for what I did, but for you and mum I'll regret what I've put you through, for the rest of my life," he whispered.

Hamish nodded, "Yes well, I've no doubt we'll get over it in time, especially now we know you're home. Were you hurt in any way?"

"No, I was treated well enough," he told him.

"What can we do for you now?" Isla asked.

"I think I just need some quiet time, to adjust, Mum, I feel disorientated."

"We should take you home with us," she insisted.

Rory shook his head, "I have to stay here, with the General."

"This is ridiculous," Isla snapped, "You are our son. We have rights. We need to know what's been going on."

"No, we don't," Hamish snapped back, "You heard the General. Do you want Rory taken away again?" Isla shook her head. She never wanted Rory to leave ever again! Hamish continued, "I think we'd better let Rory get some rest, love. We can come back tomorrow son," he decided.

"I'd like that Dad, hopefully I'll be thinking straight again by then." Hamish took Isla's arm, expecting some argument, but instead she simply nodded.

"Yes, we'll come tomorrow," she repeated meekly. Rory went back downstairs with them and saw them into their car. He waved as they drove away. Next moment, he was standing breathing in the crystal-clear air and drinking in the view out over the moors. Tears fell down his face. He had never expected to see these views ever again. Now, he was here he swore he'd never leave them again!

Next moment, Callum drew up in his land rover and leapt out, "Okay mate," he tried to ignore the tears still wet on Rory's face. Rory turned to him,

"I will be now. Look out there," he waved his arm at the view, "I thought I'd never see it again."

Callum decided to ignore the emotion, "Here, grab these," he handed over a dozen bottles of beer to Rory, then collected up a basket of food and grinned, "Mum assumed you'd not been fed all the time you were away. She's thrilled you're back and she is trying to ring Caitlyn, to give her the good news."

Caitlyn! Rory was shocked. He'd not given her a single thought for days. He turned to Callum, "Thanks mate and thank your mum for me too. Come on in."

This time, they settled in the little sitting area and Rory set his chair to see the views out of the window. Callum, let him sit quietly for a moment. Finally, Rory asked, "You had better tell me what's been happening to the Estate."

"I'll bring you up to date tomorrow, I promise but for tonight, we celebrate," he opened a beer and handed it to Rory. "You are home and safe and I couldn't be happier, believe me."

Rory's face broke into a huge smile, as he took the bottle. "Oh, now I know I'm home. This is just perfect Callum. Thank you."

Callum stayed with Rory that night as they made their way through the beers. Bonny lay at Rory's feet, content to know her Master was home. Morag had sent over bread, cheese, ham, milk, coffee and a large fruit cake. No food would ever taste as good, nor company more welcome, than Rory had that night. They both fell asleep in their chairs in the early hours. When Rory woke next morning, the sun was just rising over the hills and moors. It was a sight to behold and he sat silently, drinking it into his very soul. To think, he might never have seen this ever again! A thought came unbidden into his mind. If only Flame was here to see this with me, my happiness would be complete. Bonny who had slept beside him got up and licked his hand. Had she read his mind, Rory wondered?

Morag had spent the evening trying to find her daughter. She was terribly worried by Caitlyn's wild ways. She stayed away from home whenever possible and often at her mother's refusal to let her do so. She worked for a magazine in Inverness and socialised with her work mates. Callum had all but washed his hands of his sister and he and Morag often argued fiercely over her. Morag knew he was right, but she loved her daughter and leaned towards giving her the benefit of the doubt. As for her engagement to Rory, she had grave doubts, especially since Rory had disappeared. Caitlyn had shown very little concern for him, even the embarrassment of the party had washed over her. Now Morag despaired. Where was Caitlyn tonight? Finally, one of her friends answered her call and promised Morag to pass on the message that Rory was home. There seemed little else, Morag could do so she sighed deeply and went to bed.

Caitlyn arrived at the Stables at mid-day the following day. Rory and Callum were deep into the Estate business by now, after an early morning ramble together with Bonny. It was a moment, Rory would cherish for years. He was free, home and back out on High Tor with his closest friend and much-loved dog. His parents had paid a visit later. Isla had calmed down and simply hugged Rory, promising not to ask questions. She was so happy to have him home again. Hamish had managed a quiet word with Rory, assuring him he was there if ever his son needed him. They stayed for about an hour, assured themselves Rory had all he needed and left.

Rory was impressed by the way Callum had held the fort whilst he'd been away and told him so. The decisions he'd made had been the right ones, but Callum assured Rory he didn't want the job on a permanent basis. "I hate paperwork and I can't wait to get back out on the moors doing my own job." Rory understood. He sighed,

"Thinking of tramping the moors kept me sane; whilst I was—away," he whispered, "I did wonder, if I'd ever see them again."

Callum looked up sharply, concern clear in his eyes. "I wish you could tell me. I'm sorry, I know I mustn't ask."

"You don't know how much I want to talk about it," Rory confessed, "If I could talk to anyone, it would be you, Callum. I will say I made a mistake and caused untold trouble for a lot of people, especially those I love."

"I don't know about any of this obviously, but I do know you. You would never hurt anyone knowingly and those you love will always forgive," Callum spoke softly, and Rory felt tears in his eyes. However, before more could be said they heard a car out in the stable yard and Callum recognised his sister's VW.

"It's Caitlyn," he stood up, "I'm sure you want to be alone, so I'll get home. I can come back tomorrow, if you want me?"

Rory agreed, "Thanks Callum, see you tomorrow."

Callum made a quick get a way. He and his sister were not talking after a blazing row, about her not caring that Rory was missing. The two passed on the stairs.

Caitlyn stood in the doorway, not sure what sort of welcome she'd get. "Hi Rory, how are you? Where have you been?" she asked.

Rory was suddenly struck by guilt. He had offered marriage to this girl and now he'd betrayed her with Flame. "I can't tell you, where I've been but I'm okay. Come and sit down."

Caitlyn took the chair, Callum had just vacated. "You didn't even tell me, you were going. You didn't show for the party. It's not good enough Rory, I'm your fiancée and I was humiliated."

"I'm sorry, you must have been angry, I understand but I didn't know, I was going," he floundered for words.

"Yes, I was angry with you, but I was worried too," she lied, suddenly afraid. Surely, he still wanted her? She changed moods, stood up and walked over to him. "Oh Rory, I'm so glad you're back, it's all that matters. We can now get on with wedding plans," she leant down and kissed him, sliding onto his lap and hugging him.

Rory accepted the kiss half-heartedly, trying hard to push memories of Flame's kisses away.

"Before you make any wedding plans Caitlyn, I need some time, to myself," he begged feebly.

"Why, what's wrong? I'm lost here. Are you sick? You wanted to marry me, said you loved me, now you're distant, different. I need to know where I stand, Rory," she demanded angrily.

"I'm not sick. I apologise for all the hurt, for the party and for not being able to tell you, where I've been. Please, just give me some time to think."

"Why should I, if you won't tell me. I don't know why you disappeared. You could have been with another woman for all I know!" she cried.

Rory blanched white at the accusation, that hit home hard and guilt engulfed him again. Caitlyn bit her tongue trying to calm her anger. She still wanted Rory and all he stood for. She mustn't push him away. She drew a deep breath, "So how long do you want me to wait?" she asked, "Look Rory, I love you and want to marry you, I haven't changed my mind. I don't want us to argue either and so I'll do as you say. I'll wait until you're ready." She kissed him again.

"Thank you Caitlyn, just give me some time to sort myself out. So, tell me what's been happening with you?" he encouraged. Caitlyn sat back in her chair and began talking. Rory let her talk. This was his life now. Flame had been a brief magnificent affair, one he'd never forget, but she was right, it was over, there was no way they could ever meet again. He knew he'd never forget her, that the love he felt for her would always be deep in his very soul, never to be forgotten. Caitlyn was the woman he'd promised marriage to and he was an honourable man, he'd stand by his promise. Caitlyn was part of High Tor and his future. This was the only life he had, and he'd make the best of it. He stood up and took her in his arms. Caitlyn breathed a sigh of relief!

Chapter 11

Flame arranged a meeting with her cell members to be held at Tom and Huw's vineyard. Those who came were Yves and Gervaise as well as Tom and Huw. Flame got straight to the point as meetings were banned, so time was short. "I now have a new radio frequency and codes and am asking how you all feel about resuming operations?"

"Do you believe it's safe to do so?" asked Huw.

"It's never safe, Huw as you well know but I think we've eliminated the risk of radio calls being intercepted. I wondered about one drop to test the situation, if you are ready to take the risk."

"I'm willing," Yves nodded.

"And me as well," came from Gervaise.

"Count us in too," Tom spoke for his brother and himself.

"Thank you gentlemen, I will radio for a date and let you know. We will be extra cautious that night but if all goes well, we could be back in business."

"We all want that," Yves smiled. They dispersed singly and quietly. Whilst there, Flame arranged to transmit from one of the vineyards barns. Her next slot was tonight, so she hurried back to the cellar and collected her radio, before returning to the vineyard. She made herself comfortable in the barn. As darkness fell, a few noises came from the house and Flame saw a couple of girls arriving there. She smiled, that explained why the brothers were reluctant to invite her up here on a regular basis. Still, they had agreed to her leaving her radio up here and to transmit from here, as long as she hid everything and didn't tell them when she'd be there. That suited Flame.

At the appointed time, Flame sent her message, agreeing to another supply drop. When London replied, they gave her a date and time. Flame was excited, they were back in business! She found a broken space in the barn wall and hid her radio and books and carefully made her return to the cellar. She was totally unaware a third person had been listening in and noting the date of her next drop!

Thoughts of Rory were ever present in the cellar. Each time, she entered she was aware of his presence there. It never left her. At times, it was a comfort to be close to his love for her, but she was also conscious of the danger if she let it distract her. Thoughts of Rory would now be forced from her mind as she worked towards the next drop, she decided, but she had forgotten the long lonely nights, when he would return in her dreams and she would wake with her pillow, wet with tears.

Rory too was having problems ignoring thoughts of Flame popping into his head at inappropriate moments. His parents were well aware of his lapses and put them down to him having 'flashbacks' of something terrible that had happened to him. They were both worried but what could they do?

"If only he could talk to us, tell us what happened to him," Hamish worried.

"He insists he can't, but it's making him ill," Isla fretted.

"Do you know, I think I'll take him out on the moors for a walk, it could take his mind off things and the peace out there, may help him relax," Hamish decided. Isla thought it was a good idea and Hamish got ready to drive up to High Tor.

Rory was busy working in the office when Hamish arrived and suggested a walk. Bonny was curled up at his feet as usual. He greeted his dad warmly and willingly agreed to a walk. "You've saved my sanity. All this paperwork is from the Agricultural Ministry. These ones, I'm working on are our milk output for the month. You'd never believe how we have to count everything!"

"Oh yes, I would, I got to see them whilst you were away. I'm glad you're free for a break. I feel the need to get some fresh air in my lungs. How about we drive out somewhere then walk?"

"I'd enjoy that and so will Bonny. Help yourself to a coffee whilst I finish this form. It needs to be in the post by tonight," Rory told him.

The moors looked bleak and grey. A weak winter sun gave little light or warmth. Snow-capped mountains in the distant rose majestically, whilst a cold wind felt icy on their faces. Hamish pulled up on a hill with views of hills and valleys spread out below them. It had always been one of Rory's favourite places, Hamish remembered. Rory let Bonny out of the car and they watched her excitement as she scented rabbits. Rory breathed deeply, "Oh, this is great Dad. It's the first time I've ventured out this far since I got back."

"Shall we walk down to the river?" Hamish asked. "I've missed coming out here. I can't say Inverness has quite this appeal," his arm swept the view.

They walked in silence for a while until Hamish spotted a buzzard circling high above them. A bit further on Rory spotted a herd of deer on a nearby hillside. He and his dad had always shared a love of the wildlife on High Tor.

When they stopped for a break, they sat on some rocks and watched the river, still some distant below them.

"How are you doing now, Rory?" his dad asked casually.

"I'm okay, Dad, please don't worry about me."

"Of course I worry, so does your Mum, parents do, you know. We are concerned about what you've been through and I know you can't talk about it," he held up a hand as Rory went to protest, "But if there is something, anything I can help with, I'll always listen."

Rory frowned but remained silent. Hamish refused to give up, "How's Caitlyn?"

"She's okay, it's hard for her with me disappearing like I did and not telling her where I've been. She feels ignore and she isn't happy, but I can understand that," Rory admitted.

Hamish nodded, wasn't he and Isla feeling the same thing? When Hamish stayed quiet Rory sighed. "Whilst you're here Dad, I can tell you, I've decided to talk to Caitlyn about setting a date for our wedding."

"You have—you are?" Hamish stammered. He was shocked. For a while, he had thought this wedding wasn't going to take place. In fact, he'd sincerely hoped it wouldn't! It felt all wrong to him. Now he felt compelled to ask, "Are you sure about this Rory?"

Rory cursed, then apologised. "I know you aren't happy about me marrying Caitlyn, but I am capable of deciding for myself! I did agree to marry her before—so yes, Dad, I am sure."

Hamish tried again, "Yes, I am worried about this son. Caitlyn is very young, and she isn't happy living up on the moors. She has developed a love for city life, for the bright lights and the night life."

Rory butted in, "I'm sure, she will settle down at High Tor; once we're married." He stood up, "Please Dad, this is what I've decided, we both want it."

"I hope you're right, I'll say no more and I hope you'll both be very happy," Hamish sighed deeply. What more could he say? As far as he was concerned, this marriage was a disaster waiting to happen.

Once he'd made up his mind, Rory arranged to meet Caitlyn one evening. As much as he'd like to have made it a romantic evening, he couldn't whisk her off to Inverness for wining and dining, due to his confinement to High Tor. Instead he drove her out onto the moors and settled to talk under a million stars.

"I doubt this is the ideal place for a serious talk Cat, but it is at least somewhere quiet where we won't be interrupted," he began.

"What do you want to talk about?" Caitlyn was feeling cold out here in the dark and a little afraid, "Are you finishing with me, Rory?"

"Oh no, no, not unless—is that what you want, Caitlyn?" he gasped.

"No, of course not, I still want us to get married," she insisted.

"Why do you want to marry me Cat?" Rory wondered. "Do you really think you'll like the kind of life, we'll lead out here? Think about it seriously. We'd be living at High Tor, running the Estates. In winter, we'd be cut off for days, you know all this. It's not an easy life, is it? You've enjoyed working in Inverness, so won't you miss it?"

Just for a moment, Caitlyn hesitated. Would she be happy out here? She turned and smiled at Rory. "Of course, I know about living out here, wasn't I born and raised at Beacon Farm? I'm sure we could be happy living in the House. I love you Rory."

"Can you be sure we'd be happy, for years to come though, for that is what marriage means to me, a lifetime commitment," Rory ran a hand through his hair, "I'll be brutally honest with you Cat, I cannot let you marry me; thinking I'm head over heels in love with you, because I don't think I am. However, I did promise to marry you and I will, if you still want me after tonight. I hold you a good friend and I'd care for you. I'd treat you well and be faithful. In return, I'd expect you to respect me, live with me at High Tor and in time, bear me children," he drew breath. "The decision is yours Cat."

Caitlyn was stunned. This was the last thing she'd expected. Suddenly, Rory was being bold and decisive. He was no longer the easy-going person she had known all her life. It made her stop and think. Did she really want to be tied to him for life, out on the brooding moors? She loved Inverness and her work and friends. She loved the parties they went to, the theatres and dances. Was she really ready to give all that up? However, marriage to Rory brought even more rewards, the wealth, social position and the envy of her friends. She turned to him and smiled sweetly.

"I love you Rory, I have for years. I will marry you and hope that one day you'll love me too." She leaned into him and kissed him gently to seal the bargain. Rory found her comforting in his arms, not thrilling or passionate like—no he refused to think of HER at this moment. He kissed Caitlyn back and Caitlyn relaxed. She'd won at last. Her future was secure.

Rory pulled back and smiled, "Would you like to name the day?" he asked.

"Oh yes, how about Easter?" she wondered.

"Easter is fine by me," Rory agreed. "We have one problem. Where shall we live? I doubt the war will be over by then, so the House won't be available."

"Can't we buy a house somewhere?" she asked surprised.

"I may still be confined to High Tor by then, so no. Still there's no need, is there? Once the war is over, we'll move into the House, we just need somewhere until then. I don't suppose you'd put up with the Stables?" he asked tentatively.

"Oh no—sorry," her reply was instant. "I mean, oh this is awkward. I could ask Mum, if we could use my room, I suppose."

The idea didn't appeal to Rory either, but he shrugged. What choice did they have? "We'll ask her and hopefully it won't be long before this war ends," he decided, and it was settled. Once they were married at Easter; they would move into Beacon Farm.

Not even the Army could stop Rory leaving High Tor to get married, he thought, but to ensure there would be no problems, he went to see the General. The two were good friends now. On the long journey home from Surrey, they had talked a lot and each now respected the other. Following his own experience, Rory had grown a deep admiration for the agents sent out to France.

The General smiled, when Rory told him he was getting married. "I need to leave High Tor for the ceremony," he explained.

"Congratulations, Rory. Who is the lucky lady?" the General asked. The two were sitting in the little waiting room and a soldier appeared with a tray of coffee.

"Her name is Caitlyn and she lives at Beacon Farm," Rory accepted a cup of coffee.

"I'm happy for you and wish you both a happy life together," the General relaxed, "and I'll make sure you have no problems leaving here, on the day. How are you getting on now, after France?"

"Okay, I'm not asked so many questions now. Time passes and people forget, I suppose. Not me, let me add. I remember it all as if it were yesterday"

The General nodded, "You will of course, but you've done well, keeping it all secret. We are pleased with you. You can still talk it over with me. Is there something worrying you right now?"

Rory hesitated too long and next moment he blurted out, "Getting married to Caitlyn—there was a woman in France, Resistance, I can't forget her-oh forget I said– put it down to wedding nerves," he gulped his coffee, deeply embarrassed.

The General took time to answer before saying, "I've heard others mention this problem. More often or not, it's simply a heat of the moment situation, while under dangerous conditions. Men about to die taking pleasure while they can. It never comes to anything Rory, it can't. You met this woman and you left, that's it, over. There's no way you could meet up again. Sadly, the Resistance fighters don't survive out there for long, it's a dangerous occupation," he paused. "Unfortunately, you were more vulnerable to this, than our trained operatives. My advice is to forget her, marry your sweetheart here and live a happy life." The General refilled his coffee cup. "I'm glad you could talk about this with me. Do remember, I'm always here." They went on to discuss the war news and Rory was interested to hear the General's view. When he left, he felt a lot happier but somehow, he knew no matter what, he'd never forget Flame. As for never seeing her again, well, hadn't he come to the same conclusion?

Christmas arrived with the first heavy snow fall of the year in the Highlands. The festivities were held at Beacon Farm again with Hamish and Isla battling bad weather to join them. Rory's vanishing act was no longer a topic of conversation. Instead, talk of the wedding was in full swing. Caitlyn would be giving up her job in the New Year to take over the plans for the big day. Rory marvelled at how quickly life moved on. Only weeks ago, he'd been in France. He couldn't forget it so easily, it was all so clear in his mind, as was Flame. Just one week in his life and yet she had turned everything upside down. He wondered was she well? Was she safe? Did she miss him as much as he missed her? He had long since given up trying to forget her. He knew she was with him, to stay. He had also accepted he'd never see her again and that Caitlyn and High Tor were his future.

Caitlyn was being a model fiancée. She made time each weekend to be with him and to seek his views on the wedding. He had made her happy, he knew. He had also done the right thing by fulfilling his promise to her. All he had to do was live with his decision, stand up in church on Easter Saturday and make his vows to her. Was it that simple?

Chapter 12

The night of the expected supply drop found Flame and her cell mates camped out at the airstrip, waiting. Close by stood Gervaise's van ready to move the supplies up to the farm and to transport another agent to his new address. All around was silence, Flame noted, *but was it too quiet? Were there Germans also hiding, waiting in silence too?* Flame was tense, her orders precise, no one moves a finger until she judged it safe to do so. No one argued with her, twice before she had aborted an operation in time to save their lives. They trusted her judgement implicitly.

Finally, just ten minutes later than expected, they heard the throb of a plane's engine. Next moment, it was taxiing in front of them. No one moved even then, until Flame's voice was heard, "Let's go!"

They had two minutes to unload. Flame took the agent's arm and led him to the van, "Please wait there," she told him. Each of the men grabbed a parcel, a box or a sack and threw them in the back of the van. It was close, but all the supplies were unloaded in time and the plane took to the air and disappeared into the night sky. The two Welsh brothers vanished into the night as Flame and Yves joined Gervaise and the agent in the van. At the farm, the supplies were unloaded into a barn and hidden under straw and tarpaulins. They would be distributed in the next couple of days. Gervaise left taking the agent to his destination. Only then did Flame relax. She turned to Yves and exclaimed, "We did it!"

"Yes, we did it. It feels good," Yves smiled back, "Cup of tea?"

"Yes why not. Thanks," Flame agreed. She knew she wouldn't sleep tonight. Each drop was a mix of adrenaline, fear and excitement and after each successful drop, exhilaration and exhaustion. The two sat drinking tea in an easy-companionable atmosphere. Yves pointed out that it was Christmas next week and invited Flame to share lunch with him. Flame agreed happily before leaving to sleep in her flat.

After a sleepless night, Flame was up early next morning and out in the barn. She began sorting out the parcels from the previous night. Three would be collected and another would be delivered by Gervaise to his previous cell. A small box was left and this, she saw, was for her. She went to find Yves, who was having his breakfast. He guessed what she'd been doing, "Is everything all right?" he wondered.

"Yes, it's all fine. I just came to warn you, someone will be calling, three parcels in usual place," she advised him.

"I'll be ready. Is everything else sorted?"

"They will be, thanks Yves," she assured him. "I'll be in the flat for a while then return to town."

"Please take care of yourself," Yves asked her, and she agreed.

Back in her flat, Flame unpacked her box. It contained a new battery for her radio, another note warning her of the traitor and a small revolver and ammunition. Shivers ran down her spine. She had never carried a weapon or killed anyone. She had been trained and given weapon lessons, but this felt real and frightening. The revolver was small and lightweight, a lady's weapon. So, London now knew she was a woman, thanks no doubt to Rory! It fitted neatly into her hand. This meant London was seriously concerned for her safety. This traitor was posing a terrible threat to her and her cell mates. Flame couldn't ignore it and against her wishes, she loaded the revolver and slipped it into her pocket. She tidied up the flat, locked up and headed for the cellar. She still felt safe there.

Flame returned to the flat on Christmas Eve, ready to join Yves the next day. On Boxing Day evening, another plane drop was due and everyone was ready. It was eleven weeks now since Rory had left France, yet she felt his presence with her day and night. He never left her and foolishly, she welcomed him. She loved him still as much as ever. The situation was hopeless, he had gone and would never return, yet she relived his kisses, felt his arms about her and his body close night after night. She never wanted to forget him, she admitted, and that was the truth.

On Christmas morning, a wave of nausea hit Flame as she slipped out of bed and she gasped. It had gone as quickly as it had come and she got dressed forgetting all about it. She and Yves spent a pleasant day together but when the same thing happened again next morning, Flame fell back into bed, shocked. *Was she, could she be, of course she could be but was she?* The questions flew about her brain making her dizzy. She was stunned. If she was, what was she going to do? Did she want a baby? Yes, she did if it was Rory's child. His child would be so precious to her. For her to have a part of him would be such a blessing, but it wouldn't be easy. Look at her life, she was virtually homeless, she had only part-time work as an accountant and she was a Resistance worker! Surely, it was impossible to fit a baby into her life? Flame held her head in her hands as she sat on her bed. Her life was suddenly spinning out of control. Finally, common sense took hold of her. She only suspected she was pregnant, she didn't know for sure. There was plenty of time to make sure before she had to make any decisions. She ran a hand over her stomach, unconsciously soothing the baby, she felt sure she carried. "Oh Rory!" she sighed as small tears trickled down her face. "A baby, our baby," she called out to him as if he could hear! It was the middle of January when Flame got a doctor's appointment. He confirmed that she was pregnant. He had noted a lack of a wedding ring and treated her kindly. Flame thanked him gratefully and left. Now, she had to face up to the facts, she was going to have a baby. Yet all she felt was overwhelming happiness. She was being blessed with Rory's baby!

The Boxing Day drop had gone well, but in the New Year, news began filtering through of cells being raided and workers and agents arrested, never to be heard of again. Plane drops elsewhere were being cancelled in fear, leaving the Resistance in urgent need of supplies. Flame received a request from London to increase drops into her area. It was so dangerous she refused until she had spoken to the others.

The New Year also brought Flame a new room for her to transmit from and hide her radio and paperwork in. It was an attic room over Gervaise's shop. He and his family lived on the first floor. He had found out that she was trekking to and from the vineyard in bitter weather, in heavy snow and with increased stop-and-search attacks daily by the Germans. He and his wife were terribly afraid of having her there naturally, but they agreed, her need outweighed their fears. Flame now lived in the attic on radio days and the flat in between. Living in the cellar stopped, it was out of the question in such weather.

The cell members agreed reluctantly to the extra drops. The shortage of supplies to the Resistance was now desperate, they couldn't refuse. The drops began coming in two or three times a month, a highly dangerous number. It was only a matter of time before they were discovered by the Germans, Flame knew. Surely, the Germans must know they were landing there?

By March, Flame was five months pregnant and Yves was the first to notice. When he challenged her, she had no choice but to admit it and he was furious. He pointed out the danger she was putting herself in. With Yves knowing, Flame knew the others had to be informed. Her first decision was made, she could no longer continue as group leader. She called a meeting and told them straight. They were surprised but quickly informed her, if she felt able to continue for now, they'd support her. They said they trusted her and didn't want to lose her. Flame thanked them and agreed to continue for a short time only. She suggested Yves to take over from her at short notice, if the need arose. Everyone agreed to this and Flame went home touched by their faith in her. No one, not even Yves had asked her who the father was.

It was Good Friday when the group were trapped by a German troop at the airstrip. They were simply surrounded as the plane taxied towards them. Flame screamed, "Abort! Abort!" and everyone scattered. Flame then risked her life to wave cross arms at the plane and the pilot increased power and took off. Flame was too heavily pregnant to run, so she did the next best thing. She climbed a tree, praying the Germans hadn't brought their dogs as they would quickly know she was there. She found even climbing hard in her condition, but she got high enough to be out of sight. The first thing she looked for was Gervaise's van and it was gone. She sighed with relief. However, a disturbance had her eyes searching to see what it was. She was horrified to see Huw being dragged away by two Germans and they weren't being gentle either! Flame could have wept. Huw and his brother had been solid, dependable members of the group. There was no sign of Tom. She could do nothing for Huw or anyone else. Her cell was finished, each member in danger as they ran for their lives. She feared most for Gervaise and his family. She shuddered, thinking of his young children. As for Huw, he would soon be tortured until he gave away each of their names. Local Resistance workers were treated worse than captured English agents. Locals could name cell members and where to find them. She prayed Huw could hold out long enough for the others to leave Villenue.

Flame climbed down from her tree and began planning. The first and most important thing to do was get her radio and code books away from Gervaise's attic. It was a difficult journey into town. There were extra patrols out, obviously looking for her group, but she reached Gervaise's safely. Gervaise and his family were packing up the van as she arrived.

"I'm so sorry Gervaise," she hugged him, "Where will you go?"

"My wife has family in Paris, we'll head there," Gervaise told her. His wife was trying hard not to cry in front of her children. Her eyes, when she looked at Flame were full of fear.

"Where will you go, Flame?" Gervaise asked her.

"I haven't decided yet," Flame tried to smile. In truth, she had no idea. "I'll clear out the attic," she told him and headed up stairs.

Gervaise joined her minutes later and offered, "Flame, if you wish to come to Paris with us, we'll squeeze you in."

Flame was touched by the offer, "That's kind of you, but I still have to shift some bits from the farm," she told him. "You must leave Gervaise, save your family. Good luck, my friend." She gave him a hug. Gervaise hugged her back,

"And to you, Flame." Minutes later Flame heard the van start up and drive away. She prayed deeply for the family.

Flame hurriedly collected her few things, hid her radio and code books deep inside a bag and left by the back door. She was now on the run, a wanted criminal in German eyes. With nowhere to go, she simply had to flee or die!

Chapter 13

Ever since, Flame had taken Rory to Bear's camp in the caves, Bear had listened in to Flame's radio frequency. He had opened the package sent to her from London, read her instructions and noted her new frequency and code. After she had left, he had listened in to each transmission. When she had agreed to extra drops in her area; he had thought it madness. The Germans would quickly pinpoint her airstrip, hadn't they already done so when the Englishman had been caught?

Tonight, deep in his cave he listened in again, expecting her to confirm the drop had been successful. He waited but there was nothing and he grew concerned for her. Finally, he made a rash decision and called out to his men, "I need a car and driver, anyone volunteer?"

Two men immediately jumped up from a card game. Bear nodded, "Thanks, Rene let's go."

In the car, Bear had to admit to Rene; he wasn't sure of their destination. "We'll begin at a farm—I'm searching for a lady!"

"You are Boss?" Rene was shocked. Bear's wife and young daughter had died of a fever, a few years ago. Ever since he'd avoided women as far as anyone knew.

Bear laughed, "Sorry to disappoint you but this one is a young Resistance girl who may well be in a load of trouble tonight."

"Right you are, Boss. Just tell me where to go," Rene agreed. Only trouble he could see was driving around the countryside was extremely dangerous after curfew. Still, he and all the others would willingly do anything for Bear.

Flame was struggling, she was exhausted. Being pregnant was taking all her strength. She had walked into town to Gervaise's, now she was walking out again towards the farm, all the while trying to evade the German patrols.

As she neared the farm, her senses took over. Everything was quiet, were the Germans already here? Where was Yves, had he already left? She hoped he'd got away. The farmhouse was in darkness so she by passed it and headed straight for the barn and her flat. Once inside, she grabbed her clothes, took a blanket off her bed and tied everything into a bundle. She was too exhausted to carry any more. She still didn't know where to head for but knew it had to be as far away from here as possible.

As Flame left the flat; she waited a moment for her eyes to adjust again to the darkness. As she moved forward, a figure stood in her way and she recognised Yves. She breathed a sigh of relief, "Yves, what are you still doing here? You do know Huw was caught?"

"Yes, I know Flame, now I'm sorry it's your turn to join him"

"What do you mean?" Flame demanded, confused.

"I've protected you as long as I can. Now, time is running out for me. Unless I hand you over, I'm finished too. You I'm afraid are my ticket out of here."

"You—it's you—you're the traitor! Oh no, no, you were my friend, why oh! Why Yves?!" Flame gasped horrified.

"My Mum was French, my Dad was German. I had to choose, and I chose Dad. Where's your radio?" he demanded.

"I've hidden it of course," Flame lied, though it lay only feet away. "But Yves, your wife and children?" she wondered.

"She was English would you believe and she left me to return to her parents when war broke out," he grabbed her arm, "Enough talking, it's time to go." As he moved Flame saw the pistol in his hand. She stifled a gasp and asked,

"Where are you taking me?" as her free hand searched her coat pocket for her revolver.

"You don't need to know, start walking," he pushed her forward and she broke free of his hand.

Flame drew her revolver, "No way Yves, I'll kill you first." She spoke fiercely. She raised the gun for him to see. It was now stale-mate. They each had a gun on the other.

Yves laughed nervously, "No, I know you Flame, you'd never shoot me or anyone. Put that toy away. I will shoot you, make no mistake about that. The Germans want you alive but they'll accept you dead if need be."

Still Flame pointed the revolver at him and for the first time Yves seemed unsure. It was true Flame had never killed before but she knew this was now kill or be killed. It was also now or never, the time for words was over. Still Flame stood firm, her gun on Yves as he raised his slightly. Instinctively Flame side stepped as she'd been trained to do, just as both guns fired. Both bullets hit their targets and both of them fell to the ground, wounded.

In desperation, Flame tried to crawl away and hide, but pain tore through her lower body. Feeling with a shaking hand, she found a damp sticky mess in her side. By side stepping she'd saved herself from a bullet to the chest but even so she was badly wounded. Movement was out of the question but trying to stem the bleeding was essential she knew. She grabbed a scarf from around her neck and rolled it into a ball. She lifted her clothes and plugged the scarf into her side. She lay back on the ground knowing all was lost. There was no one to come and save her and soon the Germans would come looking for Yves. Yves too, could still be alive (she didn't know if she'd killed him) and come to finish her off. She was a sitting target, she had even dropped her revolver the moment she'd fired it. She didn't know as she lay there, that Yves was laying feet from her unconscious. Flame's bullet had in bedded in his neck and he was bleeding well.

Flame had no idea, how long she lay there as her mind kept wandering. She was still bleeding and she knew death wasn't far away. She no longer cared for herself but she shed tears for her baby. She heard her voice whispering, "Oh Rory, I'm sorry, so sorry. I love you so much and I so wanted our baby."

It was much later, when she thought she heard voices. She trembled with fear. They had to be the Germans coming for Yves. When someone shook her gently; she dragged herself half awake. A big man stood over her and she stared, who was he?

"Good girl, you are still with us. Do you remember me? I'm Bear."

"Yes, Bear," she whispered, "Bear, my radio—there—and Yves, I shot him, he's the traitor," she stammered weakly. "He shot me."

"Right, rest Flame. We'll get you somewhere safe, Rene." He called, "This is Flame, can you get her in the car?" he worried.

"I'll try Boss. We need to get out of here," he panicked, as he saw the state Flame was in.

"We will, alive or dead, we can't leave her here," he spoke bluntly, "First, I've a score to settle."

Leaving Rene to deal with Flame, he found Yves, still barely alive. He gave him a vicious kick to bring him back to his senses. "Wake up traitor and listen carefully. I'm executing you here and now for betraying some very loyal brave men—and women. Do you understand?"

Yves never spoke and Bear simply fired a bullet into his head. He quickly found Yves pistol and Flame's bag, bundle and revolver nearby. He scooped everything up and ran for the car. Flame was laid out on the back seat looking white and lifeless. "Let's go!" he told Rene, "Thanks for your help tonight. We've done well here." He told him about the death of their traitor. "I only hope we can help Flame," he murmured. He couldn't help thinking she was beyond help.

Next day was Easter Saturday. Flame lay sick and in pain, in the caves. Most of the time, she was unconscious but at others she was delirious and fighting a fever. Bear fretted as he watched her. There seemed little, he could do for her. He stayed close by, forcing sips of water into her and keeping her warm. He had been shocked to find her pregnant too, surely a ghastly mistake on her part? His men watched from a distance. To them, it was obvious she was dying but Bear was their leader and held in high regard. No one questioned his decisions.

In Scotland, Rory stood in church beside Caitlyn and vowed "to love honour and cherish her until death did them part." There was a party at Beacon Farm afterwards and if the parents of the happy couple looked a little concerned no one noticed. What they did see was a nervous groom and a bride who was the life and soul of the party!

On Monday, Rory was back to work at the Stables. He was happy enough. The only problem he'd found, was sharing Beacon Farm with everyone else. It was so crowded. He was used to his own space, had never shared a small place with others before. As for Caitlyn, she had been sweet and loving and he believed once they had the House to live in, they could make a happy life together.

Flame had somehow survived the weekend. By Monday morning, she remained the same. Bear's second in command, Boaz slipped in to see how she was. Bear stood up and stretched, "She's no better. She needs medical help, but that's impossible I know." Bear moved outside, and Boaz followed, "I know the men are unhappy, but I couldn't leave her out there, could I? She has so much information, couldn't let the Germans get her."

Boaz nodded, "I know Boss. I came to remind you, we've a drop coming in tonight."

Bear started, "Tonight, I'd forgotten. Right I'll come," he decided, but stopped again, "Let me think." He paced up and down whilst Boaz watched confused, "Yes, that's it, Flame goes out on the plane!"

"What? Oh, surely not, it's against all the rules," Boaz gasped. "She would never survive the journey either Boss, would she?"

Bear had begun pacing again. "She has no chance of surviving here, has she? And if she could reach England alive, then her chance of survival is increased." He paused, "And what can England say, once she's there? I'll write a letter to explain who she is, to go with her," he continued planning.

"Yes, Boss," Boaz nodded. No one argued with Bear. He too looked ahead, "She will need to be kept warm. Those planes are freezing." He was also thinking, this could at least solve the problem of Flame being here.

Bear nodded, relief at finding a solution, "We'll strap her tightly to a stretcher to save her being tossed about. Call the men together and we'll plan the drop. Afterwards, we'll get Flame ready to go."

Later, he sat beside Flame again. He'd done his best for her, he just hoped Flame somehow knew and would understand why he'd made the decision to send her away.

Chapter 14

It was July 1944, in the Highlands and spring was finally turning into summer. New life was evident all around High Tor and the year promised bumper crops for the war effort, thanks to Callum and Rory's management.

Life was still proving difficult for Rory and Caitlyn, staying at Beacon Farm. Rory was inclined to spend more time at the Stables than necessary. He and Bonny also spent hours out on the moors. Living so close to people was new to him and he did try to adapt, appreciating it was him alone who struggled. Caitlyn was quiet now, missing her work and friends and yes, the wild parties she loved. There was no sign of a baby yet, much to his regret but he accepted it was early days. If only the war would end, he sighed so he and Caitlyn could move into the House!

In Edinburgh, Flame sat up in her hospital bed and cradled her son. It was the first day of August and sunlight streamed through the window to her side. She had been here three months now. The journey on the plane had almost killed her, she had been told. She remembered nothing about it. Apparently, she had caused an enormous panic when the plane landed on the outskirts of High Tor. The General had been woken up and had accompanied her to hospital. He read the note Bear had pinned to her and gazed at her in surprise. So this was the woman who had rescued Rory, he mused. In his book she deserved a chance then, for doing just that, but how did he explain her injuries to the hospital? In the end, he simply quoted official secrets and told them she was French and had suffered a fire arm accident. He couldn't even tell them her name and calling her Flame would have needed more explanations.

Flame was examined, and the General told her injuries were old and severe and her chance of survival slim. As for her pregnancy, her baby was in a critical state.

The General had gasped, "Baby!" He recovered quickly and thanked the doctor, "Can I just say this is one very brave woman. Please do what you can for her."

"We always do," the doctor assured him and for the next few days Flame underwent treatment, first to stabilise her condition, then to operate. The bullet had shattered her femur bone and pelvis. How her child had survived, even the doctors couldn't say.

For the first few days, the General stayed with Flame. When she became conscious long enough, he quietly explained who he was and told her she must not mention her Resistance work whilst here. He was also able to tell her where she was and how she came to be here. Even feeling as ill as she did; somehow, Flame believed this man and trusted him. She did as he said.

Flame became a celebrity in the hospital. She had told them her name was Yvette, so she became known as Yvette the French girl who had been injured in a bombing. The only problem for everyone was Flame only spoke French and just a couple of doctors and a nurse could converse with her. The General was therefore called upon to be her translator. He was spending a lot of time with her and he genuinely liked her. Two men arrived from London to question her and she answered all their questions. Her information was of great interest to London but they were at a loss as to what to do with her. Once again, the General was given the job of watching her. Meanwhile, he had suspicions of his own about her baby. He was no mathematician but even he could work out when Rory had been in France and hadn't he admitted to 'knowing' a French girl!

It was weeks later, that the doctors decided to deliver Flame's baby early by caesarean section and her son was born. The damage to her pelvis made a natural birth impossible. As she held her son, she had never been happier. If only Rory was here with her sharing her joy. By now, she knew just how near to Rory she was, yet he'd never know he was the father of a son! At night, she wept for him all over again, knowing even here she had no way of seeing him.

The two men from London returned a few days later and asked Flame if she was willingly to work for Intelligent over here? When she asked what she'd be expected to do, they told her nothing more strenuous than reading French documents and adding any information, she had on the people and places named in them. Flame agreed. She was so grateful to them for looking after her that she was pleased to be of help. She had nearly died, yet here she was, alive, getting better and she had her son! She had named him Pierre. She owed them so much.

It was the beginning of September, when Flame was finally told that the doctors believed, she was well enough to leave hospital. The General immediately, arranged with London to provide a flat for her. As she would need further outpatient treatment, one was found near to the hospital. She would be paid a small salary for her Intelligence work and London would cover the rent. It would be a massive change of lifestyle for Flame, but she determined to make the best of it. She would be able to work from home and care for Pierre. The General promised to keep in close touch with her and help her where necessary. He was full of admiration for this brave young girl. Never far from his mind was the fact, she had saved Rory; yet he never mentioned Rory's name to her. As for Pierre each time he saw him, he found himself seeing Rory in his eyes. He must be imagining it, he told himself. It was none of his business anyway.

The General did worry about Flame. She was alone in a strange city, she had no friends, no family and her English was almost non-existent. And she had a new baby to care for. Rory was the obvious person to ask if he'd help her, be a friendly face for her, but Rory was married. The General had no reason to meddle, he told himself, but Rory spoke her language, he knew all about France and what she'd been through. Rory was sworn to secrecy the same as Flame. He was ideal for her and he could teach her English. Surely, if he asked London to agree to the two meeting, there could be no objection? He decided to ask and London agreed. They had no objection. In fact, they were downgrading Flame's status. She would continue to work for them as her work had been excellent and of great interest to them, but the war was slowly coming to a close and they had new plans to make for; when it ended.

Still, the General hesitated. Would he be doing the right thing bringing the two together? Even, if he was right about Pierre—well, surely Rory had a right to know – but if he was wrong? He decided to approach Flame first.

The General arrived one week after he had moved her to the flat. He had seen it was nothing special, just a one bedroom, one sitting room and bathroom with a tiny kitchen area off the hallway. However, Flame was happy with it, he could see and very grateful to be given it. They settled down with a coffee and the General brought up the question of her having English lessons.

Flame was thrilled. "I would love some lessons," she exclaimed.

"I may have someone in mind Flame. Do you remember rescuing an Englishman?" he asked tentatively.

Flame gasped, "Of course, I do—Rory!"

"Yes, that's him, I wondered about asking him to teach you. What do you think?" the General asked.

The colour drained from Flame's face as he watched, and he had to ask, "Flame, I need to know—forgive me—is Rory Pierre's father?"

Flame's head shot up and she stared fiercely. "Yes, he is," she nodded.

"Then, how do you feel about him coming here?" the General wondered, "Does he even know about Pierre?"

"No, he doesn't but I'd like him to know," she admitted. "I would love to see him again."

Now the General was in a fix. "Flame, I'm sorry, Rory has married since coming back."

"He married his fiancée?" she whispered. "Oh Rory," it was a bitter cry.

"I'm sorry. Perhaps we won't ask him to come then," he decided but Flame shook her head, "No, I want him to come. I want him to know about his son. He has a right to know," she insisted heatedly.

"Think about it, Flame. What good would it do anyone?" he asked but Flame was adamant, she wanted to see Rory and the General sighed heavily. He had made a mistake here and opened a can of worms. He gave in, "Very well, I'll speak to him, but if he says no—I'm not pushing him. I can only see trouble here," he informed her.

The General approached Rory, a week later. He had put off coming as long as he could, he admitted to himself. It was a glorious day at the end of September and Rory had started work early hoping to escape to the moors, once work was complete. He welcomed the General warmly, the two being close friends by now.

"I've come to ask you something Rory," he began.

"I'll stop you there!" Rory told him, "I'm not interested in anymore jaunts for you."

"I seem to remember we had nothing to do with your 'jaunt'," he smiled, "No this is different. I'll get straight to the point. You will remember Flame, the girl who saved you?"

Rory leapt from his chair, "Flame! What about her?" he demanded.

"Sit down and I'll tell you," the General spoke softly. He'd been amazed by Rory's re-action. "Flame is in Edinburgh. She was shot and injured in France."

"How badly injured?" Rory demanded.

"She has recovered and is out of hospital. She is doing some paperwork for the Intelligence services. However, she has little knowledge of English and I've suggested you as a possible teacher. How do you feel about that?"

How did he feel? Rory gasped, he was shocked and amazed. His heart was bursting with joy. He had a chance to see Flame again. He dragged his thoughts together. "How often would you need me? I'm very busy here and Edinburgh is a long journey."

"I suggest once a week and we'll provide a car and driver for you. It's a lot to ask, I know. I'll give you time to talk it over with your wife."

Caitlyn! He hadn't given her a thought. "How much can I tell her?"

"No one must know Flame is Resistance, Rory. We'll simply say you are needed as a French interpreter in a civilian position," the General decided.

"Why did you think of me?" Rory wondered. "Surely, you have other French speakers more qualified than me?"

"Not one who knows Flame or who Flame trusts. You fit the bill well."

"You mean Flame knows; you are asking me and she agrees?" once again Rory was stunned.

"Yes of course, we had to clear it with her first," the General nodded.

Rory nodded slowly, "Then, I'm happy to agree. I hope I can help her. I do owe her a lot, so I'll do my best."

"Thank you Rory. I'll fix a date for your first visit," the General stood up and Rory went downstairs with him. At the bottom the General hesitated, "Oh, I forgot to mention. Flame has a baby, a lovely little boy. Goodbye Rory, I'll be in touch." He told him and all but ran away, calling himself all kinds of a coward, but he had found it impossible to tell Rory about his son!

Rory stood transfixed to the spot. Flame had a baby, a boy! He was choked, reeling with shock. He climbed back up to the office and sat very still. Why was he upset, he wondered? Hadn't he married Caitlyn, so why wouldn't Flame get on with her life too? Next moment, the knowledge he'd soon see her again; had his heart beating a tattoo. He couldn't wait. All he had to do now was tell Caitlyn and his family. That could be interesting!

Chapter 15

Five days later, Rory knocked on Flame's door in Edinburgh, his arms full of books provided by the General. Flame had waited nervously, excited one moment but scared the next. What would Rory do, sweep her up in his arms or keep her at arm's length? She had to remember he was married, yet she screamed out against it. How could he marry after all they'd had together?

Flame opened the door, hesitantly. Once he was inside, there could be no going back, she knew. Had the General even told him about Pierre, she wondered?

For a moment, they simply stared at each other then silently Flame stepped aside and Rory walked in. "This way," she indicated the little sitting room where Pierre was asleep in a cradle.

"This is Pierre. Did the General mention him?" she asked nervously.

Rory had been drinking in the sight of Flame, savouring her nearness to him but now he turned to the baby. "He mentioned; you had a son." He put down the books on a table and turned to the baby. Dark hair and dark eyes, he noted a small mouth and straight nose. Suddenly, he was shaking. This was the baby in the photo displayed on his mother's mantel-piece and the truth hit him. Pierre was the splitting image of himself, as a baby!

"Flame, no, oh no!" he groaned and his legs gave way. He sat down on the settee. "Tell me, please," he begged.

"Meet your son," she whispered as tears filled her eyes. If Rory rejected her, she could accept it. If he denied his son, it would destroy her. By now, Rory had eyes only for his son and he knew without a shadow of doubt, Pierre was his. He reached out and touched the tiny hand. This was his son! Next moment, he was in Flame's arms and tears fell as they both cried. His lips crushed hers. Flame revelled in him, touching him, returning kiss for kiss. Time passed unnoticed as they made up for lost time, yet it was as if they'd never parted. They were rudely interrupted by a loud wail. Pierre was awake, demanding his mother's attention. Flame broke free and moved to pick him up. Rory took her arm, "May I hold him?" he asked, and she nodded.

Rory sat on the settee with Pierre in his arms, marvelling at his son. His son! Again, he turned to Flame, "He's—wonderful," he whispered as Pierre's eyes fixed on him, curious to know who this man was. "Oh Flame, I had no idea, I never thought—when we—I put you at risk, I'm so sorry."

"Neither of us thought, did we? We were carried away– by love– weren't we?" she smiled. "It was a shock when I found out, but such a good one, in the end."

"You've had to cope with so much alone, haven't you? I know very little; won't you tell me from the beginning. How were you shot?" He shifted slightly and moved Pierre closer in his arms. Happily, Flame snuggled closer to Rory and sighed, "It was an awful experience. You will remember when you were captured I told you it was because we had a traitor? Well it was Yves, my second in command. He tried to capture me, hand me in to the Germans. We both had guns and we shot each other at the same time. Not a good idea," she laughed, finally putting it behind her. "Bear rescued me, you remember him? He was the leader of the group who flew you out, the men in the caves."

Rory nodded, he remembered. He was mesmerized listening to her story. Even sitting here, beside her was breath-taking. Flame continued, "Bear took the decision to fly me out to England, no Scotland," she amended. "It was against all the rules but he saved my life and my baby—our baby. I nearly died. I'd fractured my leg and pelvis and even now no one knows how Pierre survived it. I had to have a caesarean as my pelvis couldn't take a normal birth. I walk with a limp and always will, but I owe everything to the doctors here." She was tearful reliving it all and Rory's eyes filled with tears too. "I owe them my gratitude too, for saving you both," he glanced down at Pierre and pulled Flame closer with his other arm. It was a moment to savour, sitting close as a family unit for the first time. Next moment, the silence was shattered by Pierre giving another loud wail. Flame took him from Rory, "He's hungry, I'm afraid. I need to feed him, so I'll take him in the bedroom," she decided.

Fascinated by all these new experiences Rory asked without thinking, "May I watch?"

Flame actually blushed, but nodded, "I don't see, why not." It was only then Rory realised how she would feed Pierre. "Oh, I'm so sorry, please excuse me," he gasped, blushing himself.

Flame laughed merrily, "Come on, there's no real reason why you shouldn't be there?"

Minutes later, Rory was watching enthralled as Pierre hungrily suckled Flame's breast. He had never seen a sight more beautiful. Here was the woman he loved, feeding his son. His son! It was only just sinking in.

When Pierre was satisfied, Flame changed his nappy and tucked him into his cradle in the bedroom. "We can talk in the sitting room without disturbing him," she decided. Minutes later, Pierre slept once again and they crept out.

Flame made them, cups of coffee and they settled back in the sitting room. Flame began by asking, "What happened to you when you got back?"

Rory frowned. He had to tell her the truth he knew. She deserved nothing less. "There's no easy way to tell you Flame, I married Caitlyn."

Flame nodded, "The General told me. Are you happy?" she whispered. "Oh, don't answer that, I've no right to ask." When Rory remained silent, she added, "Let's be honest here. Neither of us expected to meet up again, did we? We simply had a brief— encounter."

"No, that's not true! We met and fell in love and I still love you, Flame. We didn't have sex, we made love and to know Pierre was conceived of that love thrills me." He ran a hand through his hair, "If only, I'd known you were pregnant."

Flame was close to tears, loving him for his words about Pierre. "We were separated by war. There was no way I could tell you, nothing you could have done if I had," she admitted. "Oh Rory, I loved you so much and when I found out I was carrying your baby, I swore I'd love him and protect him, because he was yours. I expected to raise him alone. I never dreamed we'd meet again."

Rory pulled her into his arms and hugged her, "Now we have met again, we can deal with it. I'll never let you go again. I'll support you and Pierre—he needs to know his dad," he vowed.

"Stop, oh stop, Rory. You have a wife—what on earth will she have to say about us, Pierre and me?" She pushed him away.

Rory faced her, he looked pale. "Let me explain about Caitlyn. When I got back from France, I knew I didn't love her. I have never felt for her, what we had and that's the truth, but before I went to France I had agreed to marry her, so I felt honour bound to see it through. I never expected to see you again Flame, now I'm so sorry." In fact, he was feeling sick, just thinking about it. "I did tell Caitlyn I didn't love her, but she still wanted to go ahead. If only, I'd called off the wedding!"

Flame remained silent, absorbing all he'd said and she believed him. How could she blame him? She had never expected to see him again either had she? "What do we do?" she wondered.

"Do we have to do anything right away?" Rory asked, "I'll be here every Tuesday, thanks to the General. I can't believe, he knew but never told me. Today has been a shock, but a wonderful shock to me. We can make any decisions later. Oh Flame, I feel I'm dreaming, being here with you."

Rory took her in his arms again and kissed her tenderly. Flame revelled in his arms and his kisses before saying, "I expect nothing from you Rory. I thought I'd be raising Pierre alone."

"I want to be there for you both, for my son to know me. I've no idea what the future will hold," he frowned again, as reality sunk in.

"None of us does, do we?" Flame wriggled closer to him, "No more words, please will you kiss me again?"

Rory duly obliged, kissing her with a passion he'd never expected to feel again. He felt whole, fulfilled and so happy. As for Flame, she had never been so happy. Rory was here in her arms, promising to be part of her and Pierre's life. She clung to him, never wanting to let him go.

Finally, Rory broke free. "The car will soon be back for me," he told her, "and I haven't taught you any English, not that I'm complaining" he grinned, "However, I do have to fulfil my duties. I brought some books with me, so will you have a look at them in the week and we'll go through them next Tuesday."

Flame agreed, "I do want to learn," she assured him.

"Can I say goodbye to Pierre?" Rory asked.

Flame nodded and whilst they waited for the car, they sat down together beside his cot and watched him sleeping. They held hands together and kissed. "I cannot believe, you are here," Flame whispered.

"Fate couldn't keep us apart. We were meant to be together," Rory smiled at her.

"Oh, I want to believe that," Flame sighed.

It had been a wonderful day for them both, but for Rory it had changed his life. Today, he had not only found Flame again, he had discovered he had a son. A son! As the car sped back to High Tor; Rory's life would never be the same again.

Chapter 16

Over the next couple of days Rory was questioned about 'the French girl'. Not so much by Caitlyn, who showed little interest, but by Morag and his parents. He managed to answer confidently enough. "She was French and had somehow been injured. She is connected to the War Office because the General is her boss." At no time did he mention Pierre. His mother and Morag appeared satisfied with his answers but not so his dad. He kept returning to the lessons and probing about Flame. Rory wondered what his dad suspected. Had Rory slipped up in his answers somehow? However, the one person who had remained quiet about the subject was Callum. Now, he suddenly turned up at the Stables office one morning and settled in the chair opposite Rory. Rory looked surprised as Callum helped himself to a coffee. Callum spoke first, "So what have you got yourself involved in this time?" he asked.

Rory stared at him, "What are you talking about?" he asked.

"This French girl, what's her name by the way?" Callum demanded.

Rory was shaken, "You want to know her name?" he struggled. He always called her Flame. "Her name's Yvette," he suddenly recalled.

"Yvette, that's a pretty name. So, she does exist then? How was she hurt?"

"What is this all about, Callum?" Rory demanded. He had to go on the attack here, take control of the conversation.

"I find it hard to believe you are teaching English lessons. There are plenty of teachers in and around Edinburgh, without involving you," Callum insisted.

Rory shrugged non-chalantly, but he was worried. "The General asked me. He is in charge of her. What's worrying you Callum? Is it your sister?"

"Partly, she's unhappy Rory, but it's more than that. I get worried when the General is involved with you. I need to know if you are putting yourself in danger again"

"No, of course I'm not. I wouldn't," Rory insisted, "I am teaching a French girl, English. You have nothing to worry about."

"I do worry. I have ever since you disappeared. And I worry for Caitlyn."

"What about Caitlyn?" Rory was getting annoyed about being cross-examined in this manner.

Callum flushed, embarrassed, but he couldn't stop now, "It's as if the spark has gone out of her. I know she's unhappy, but she won't speak about it to me. Oh, this is awkward. She is my sister and I'm worried."

Rory nodded. "Very well, I'll take on board what you've said about Caitlyn and I'll talk to her. You have no need to worry. I married her, and I'll always stand by her."

"Thanks, I'll leave you to sort it out," Callum leapt up. "The Vet's coming to one of our cows. I have to get back." He was eager to get away. He was embarrassed by the conversation, but he'd been worried about Caitlyn and the General. Why he felt the man spelt trouble, he couldn't say.

As soon as Callum had left Rory groaned and put his head in his hands. Meeting up with Flame again had been wonderful, she was the love of his life, but now reality hit him hard. Every conversation he had with his wife, his brother in law and parents was fraught with lies and fear he'd slip up. He hated deception in any form yet now he was in the thick of it!

Rory tried to face the facts. He had a wife who deserved better of him. He had Flame, not a mistress, yet, but the woman he loved, and she had born him a son! She deserved better too. He was in a mess; a terrible fix and he had no idea how to sort it out. As for Callum, Rory wasn't surprised he'd sensed his pre-occupation. They had been close for many years. Callum knew Rory well and until now, the two had shared all their thoughts and feelings. If he hadn't been married to Callum's sister, he could well have confided in Callum. As for Caitlyn, the guilt he was feeling over his love for Flame had just increased fourfold; thanks to Callum. He also admitted he'd noticed Caitlyn's withdrawal into herself. He would talk to her about it, he decided.

Something else had occurred to him; whilst Callum was talking. He had no idea of Flame's surname. Nor did he know, under what name Pierre had been registered on his birth certificate. He'd have to find out next Tuesday. Oh, he couldn't wait to see his son again! Whatever else happened, he would never abandon Flame and Pierre, of that he was certain.

Whilst Rory fretted over their situation, Flame was on cloud nine. She had never been happier in her life, which up to now had been one of loneliness and hardship. As she went about her chores, she found herself singing. As she fed Pierre, she told him about his "Papa." It was all so wonderful. How could her life have changed so quickly? She was sensible enough to know there were problems ahead, even tears for her if Rory chose to stand by his wife, but for now she would hold on to his promise to care for them.

When the General called in, he could see the difference in her. He noted her glow and shiny eyes and he felt like grinning. No harm done here, he mused, I wonder how things are at High Tor. He had brought Flame, more documents to work on and after he'd had coffee and a chat, he left her to start work on them. The officers from London were very pleased with her observations and the information, she could provide. As Pierre slept beside her she read the first report. By the time, she reached the third one; however, a code name hit her. It was Bear! She read on fast. Bear had been captured, along with two of his men. Oh no, she cried, not Bear! Memories of the man flooded back. She relived the night she'd slept in his caves, under his protection. He had been responsible for getting Rory out of France and he'd raced to save her, the night she'd been shot. He had broken the rules by putting her on a plane, to safety. Resistance workers lived and died in France, yet here she was, alive and well with a beautiful baby, all thanks to Bear. Tears fell down her face as she remembered, and she sent up a heart-felt prayer for Bear to somehow survive against all the odds.

When Rory suggested one evening that he and Cat have a chat, Morag immediately disappeared into the kitchen. Callum decided it was time to check on his cows, leaving Caitlyn looking surprised.

Rory got straight to the point. "I'll not lie to you, Callum tells me how unhappy you are, and I want to know, if it's true, what I can do to help?"

"Oh, I'm sorry. I hope you haven't worried about me?" Caitlyn gasped.

"Of course, I'm concerned. Can you tell me what's wrong?"

Caitlyn hesitated, "As a child, I dreamed of being married to you," she blushed, "But now it's nothing like I imagined. I expected to live an exciting life in the House."

"Well the war is coming to an end and soon we could be living there," Rory mused, thinking deeply. He didn't like living here either!

Caitlyn continued now she'd started. "I guess I'm lonely. I enjoyed my life before we married. I enjoyed my work on the magazine. I had friends there to socialise with, drinks after work and parties. I must sound very selfish Rory and I'm sorry."

"No, it's not selfish, that sounds absolutely normal for a young girl. It seems we did marry too soon, for you," he sighed. "What can we do right now though, to sort this out?"

"There's nothing, we can do. I agreed to marry you. You warned me, I was too young, but I didn't listen. I will simply have to get on with it," she whispered.

"But that won't solve anything, and I don't want you to be unhappy," Rory decided, "Is there anything that would help right now?"

Caitlyn paused uncertain and Rory encouraged her, "Go ahead."

"Well, a friend rang me today to tell me there is a job going on the magazine, and asked if I'd like to apply," Caitlyn told him.

"And you'd like to?" Rory was surprised, "But then you'd have to be in Inverness, all week!"

"No, that's the best bit. This job is part time, just two days a week," Caitlyn was excited, "I would have to drive up on Monday, work Tuesday and Wednesday and come home Wednesday night." She stopped realising she'd pushed too hard. "I know it's not what I agreed to before we married, and I didn't believe I'd be able to apply. I'm sorry Rory, but you did ask."

Rory remained silent for what seemed a long time to Caitlyn. He was a little shocked by her honesty. Finally, he nodded, "Okay, thanks for telling me all this. Give me time to think it through, will you?" Caitlyn nodded as hope was born. Rory suddenly asked, "Just a thought, will you give up work, if you become pregnant?"

The question shocked Caitlyn. She frowned deeply and muttered, "I suppose so."

Rory too was shocked by her re-action. He knew instantly that Caitlyn did not want to start a family. Was that why? Had she been preventing? He shook visibly and knew in that moment, he never wanted children with her either! "I see, so you don't want a family either! Why on earth did you want to marry me? Why did you agree to us having a family? You were the one— oh Caitlyn." This was too much for Rory. The marriage was a disaster and he blamed himself for going ahead with it. He'd known she was too young, his father had constantly warned him and just look at the mess they were all in now, including Flame!

Caitlyn bowed her head. "I'm sorry, Rory," she whispered.

Anger would solve nothing here, Rory decided. He took a couple of deep breaths then asked, "Tell me about this job; you've been offered."

"It's in advertising, the same department I worked in before. I know the work well," she told him.

"And this is really what you want?" Rory asked.

Caitlyn nodded, and so did Rory. "You better apply then," he told her.

"Do you mean it? You won't mind me working?"

"Oh, I wouldn't go that far, but in this, well, I'd rather have you here happy half the week than miserable all week," he grinned. "I just hope you will be happy, Caitlyn."

"Thank you Rory, I'm sure I will be," she smiled.

Rory left the room and called to Bonny. In no time he and his dog were out on the moors. Walking at night out here always cleared his mind but not this time. In no time, he was feeling sick and ashamed of himself. Caitlyn had deceived him by not wanting children, but what about him? He was hiding secrets from her too and everyone else he knew. He was lying to people every day. He had no right to be angry with Caitlyn when he himself was leading a double life. It was late when he eventually returned to Beacon Farm and he was still in turmoil.

Chapter 17

For the next few months, Rory and Caitlyn's life fell into a new routine. Each Monday afternoon Caitlyn drove off to Inverness, ready to work on Tuesday and Wednesday. There was no doubt in Rory's mind that she was much happier. On Tuesday's Rory was collected by car and spent time with Flame and Pierre. English lessons were now firmly undertaken, and Flame was excelling at speaking it, if not in the written word. Both Rory and the General were delighted with her progress. Rory had been humbled to find his name on Pierre's birth certificate and now supported him with an allowance each month.

By the end of November, Rory was planning to spend time with them both over the Christmas period. The day they had finally given in to their feelings for each other and made love, Rory had settled down with Flame afterwards and talked for the first time about their situation. He admitted he felt honour bound to stay with Caitlyn, his marriage vows weighing heavily on his conscience. He had sworn, he loved only her and he would always support her and Pierre, but he could not take the relationship further for now. "I love you so much Flame and I know I'm treating you badly, please forgive me. If you want me to leave now and never return, I'd quite understand, just tell me."

Flame was naturally sad at the prospect of always being 'Rory's secret' but accepted it. She loved him so much she'd take whatever crumbs he offered her, for now. However, she knew time would soon change things. Already, she could see he was riddled with guilt over their affair and she felt saddened for him.

Christmas was a happy time for everyone at High Tor. It was impossible for Rory to get away to see Flame; but he'd organised some extra days visit the week before. That had been when they opened their presents. Rory had loved every minute of that day. Flame spent a quiet Christmas day alone. This was what being a mistress meant, she realised! In some ways she was angry with herself for being so weak, where Rory was concerned but she loved him more than ever and enjoyed him when she had the chance.

New Year saw in the year 1945 and the war dragged on for its final months. Flame felt the first flickers of fear over her position here in Scotland for when it ended. What would happen to her and Pierre? Did she have any rights to stay here? She felt unable to force Rory to take on full responsibility for them. Meanwhile, as spring turned to summer Rory began to make plans for Pierre's first birthday in July. He had such plans, even Flame caught his excitement. However, events overtook them when in June the war officially ended. Celebrations were held everywhere, and Rory organised a party for all the Estate workers on High Tor. Their happiness grew every time a worker returned home from serving their country to resume working on the Estates.

By the end of June, both Rory and Flame received official letters thanking them for their 'war efforts'. Rory's pointed out his linguistic work was no longer required and hence no car would be available in future. Flame's was more in depth. It thanked her for the important documentation, she had provided for the War Office but with the end of the war it was no longer required. It went on to explain the rent on her flat would cease to be paid on the 31st July. She and her son were offered a flight back to France at the War Office's expense. If she decided to remain in Scotland, she would have to apply for permission to stay.

Flame flew into a panic. What was she to do? For a moment, she couldn't think and when Pierre gave a cry wanting her attention, she shoved the letter in her pocket and went to deal with him. At eleven months, he was a strong sturdy boy and very active. He kept Flame busy from morning until night these days. It wasn't until he was asleep that night, that Flame had time to re-read the letter. It was quite straight forward, she assessed. She had the choice of returning to France or applying to stay. She had to choose because from the end of July, she'd be homeless. She wondered about getting work and a place of her own here but could she with Pierre to care for? She knew no one, who could baby sit for her. Surely, the same applied to France. She had no one to go to out there. Was she then reduced to begging Rory to find her accommodation? He would, she knew without a second thought but was that fair to him?

Flame tried to assess their relationship, dispassionately. Oh, she loved him deeply and knew she always would. The fact Rory loved her too, she had never doubted, but he had a wife and he'd made it clear to her; he wasn't prepared to leave her. He was so honourable and he was putting vows, he'd made to Caitlyn before her. She could see it troubled him, that guilt was burning in him because he had a mistress. She had to ask, would he change, if she waited? Would she ever have a future with him? She was certain, he'd provide for Pierre but what about her? Was she destined to be 'Rory's mistress, his secret life' forever? The price to her was beginning to look too high. All her life, she had fended for herself. When she'd discovered she was pregnant, she had faced the fact she would have to raise him alone. Her heart was breaking. Was she really considering leaving here and returning to France? Could she do it? Could she deprive Rory of his son? How cruel was that? Yet by being with them both, Rory was already crippled with guilt. And the money needed to support them, had to come from his accounts. How long before he couldn't face the strain anymore and she'd be alone again?

Flame felt the tears running down her face. She hadn't realised, she was crying. Her heart was breaking, she couldn't leave him. Nor could she subject Pierre to an unknown future in France. She had to stay, yet she felt weak and helpless at putting herself in such a vulnerable position. She dried her eyes and went to bed. Early next morning, before Pierre woke, she was up. Sometime during the night, she had made her decision.

Next morning, the General made an unexpected appearance. He immediately noted her drawn looks and pink eyes. Flame invited him in. She always loved seeing him. The General immediately scooped Pierre up into his arms. "How are you, young man?" he tickled him and Pierre squealed happily.

"He's teething again," Flame explained, "and he's found his feet and is into everything! His poor mother is exhausted." She led him into the sitting room, "Would you like some tea?"

The General set Pierre down and sat on the settee, "I'd love one, please." He waited until Flame had made some tea before asking, "I was concerned about you. I assume you've had a letter?"

"Yes, it came yesterday," she smiled at the General. How kind, he was. He was always thinking of her. He had been so good to her through everything that had happened here. He was the nearest, she could imagine a father would be.

The General was watching Pierre playing, "He's grown since I was last here." He smiled, "I've brought you the papers needed to apply for residency here, Flame."

Flame shook her head sadly, "They won't be needed, I'm afraid. Thank you General, but I've decided to return to France," she whispered.

"You have, oh Flame, why?" he looked shocked.

Flame thought deeply, "There are a number of reasons," she hesitated.

"Perhaps, you'd rather not tell me," the General sighed, "I won't ask. Oh, I'm going to miss you so much. I've never told you but I'm a lonely man Flame and knowing you, well I've grown very fond of you. I sensed you were lonely too," he stopped embarrassed. "Goodness! Where did all that come from?"

Tears fell down Flame's face and she leant across and gave him a hug. "I'll miss you too, so much. Yes, I guess I've been lonely all my life and knowing you has been lovely. As for my leaving, I'll tell you why. You must have realised Rory and me are lovers. We were in France, hence Pierre and have been again here. I love him so much, but he's married. I've had to take a good look at my life. In ten years' time, will I still be Rory's secret? Will Pierre not be acknowledged as his son? I can't face all that, so I need to put Pierre first now, before we drift into a life that's not good for anyone."

"I admit, I'm shocked," the General gasped, "I always expected Rory to sort out his marriage and marry you."

"He's never mentioned marriage to me," Flame told him sadly. "He says he loves us, he pays Pierre an allowance but that's it. He can't leave his wife."

"Oh Flame, The man's a fool. I'm so sorry. I know he'll be devastated over losing you both, especially Pierre. He adores him."

"But not enough, it would seem. I am sorry to take his son, but I have decided. I thought I'd just slip away, not make a scene. Could you arrange the flight, I was offered?" she wondered.

The General nodded, "Yes, I can. I also have a form for that here. I do wish, I could stop you but I'll accept your decision. However, I'm going to impose some conditions on you, I'm afraid. I will want to know your address when you reach France and how you both are. I shall come and see you regularly. I never want to lose you," he added shyly. "Where will you go? I haven't asked if you know someone you can stay with?"

"No there's no one out there. I'll try Paris and look for work. I know it's going to be hard to begin with, but my life has never been easy. We'll do okay." She tried to smile.

The General was shocked all over again. Flame would be alone with a child, no home and no work, in a city recovering from war! He was frightened for her.

Flame then turned to face him, "I'll agree to your conditions only if you agree to never tell Rory where we are," she insisted.

The General was trapped. He had considered telling Rory where she was at a later date, but now he simply nodded. "If that is what you want, okay. I'll sort out a flight for you and let you know, when it is. I'll also drive you to the airport." It was best he knew where she was, so he would have to keep her whereabouts secret.

"Thank you, you have been so kind to us," she was upset again.

"It has been my pleasure Flame to know you. I shall come over and visit you, I promise," he assured her.

"I'd really like that General," she smiled, "and so will Pierre," she smiled as Pierre tried to climb the General's leg. They both laughed.

One week later, the General arrived to take Flame and Pierre to the airport. For the past few days, Flame had worried about Rory turning up at the flat, but he hadn't been able to get away from High Tor. She knew she would never see him again. This break really was final.

Unable to sleep on the last night, she sat up and wrote Rory a heart-breaking letter. She handed it silently to the General, who read the name on the envelope and nodded. He slipped it in his pocket, "I'll see he gets it," he promised sadly, "and I have an envelope for you. There's enough money there to keep you in a small hotel for a couple of weeks. Just until, you find somewhere for yourselves."

"Oh no, I couldn't take your money!" Flame insisted, embarrassed.

"It's not mine. I applied to the office for you," he lied blatantly. Flame accepted it gratefully and asked him to thank, 'the office'.

As the General watched the two pass through the airport to take off, his heart was sinking. What would happen to them?

It was the following day when the General turned up at High Tor. Rory was in the office at the Stables having a meeting with Callum and two men from the hunting, shooting and fishing organisation they dealt with. He was surprised to see the General. Although, they had kept in touch, the General hadn't been out to High Tor for quite a while.

The General apologised, "I'm sorry Rory, I've obviously chosen the wrong moment."

"Well yes, I am busy just now, but if you wouldn't mind waiting?" he felt a flicker of fear. The General and Flame were connected in his mind. He turned to the two men, "Would you excuse me for a moment, I'll just show the General where to wait." He hurried the General out and across into the sitting room. "What's wrong? Is it Flame?" he demanded.

"Flame is well and so is Pierre. Deal with your meeting Rory. I'll wait here until you are free," he sat down, determined to wait, however, long it took.

Far from satisfied, Rory returned to his office. Some instinct was alarming him. Callum had watched quietly. He too, was worried. What was the General up to now? Somehow, he was always at the bottom of trouble where Rory was concerned. The meeting continued, however, and figures were raised, discussed and altered before being accepted by both sides. In the end, High Tor won a great contract but Rory's mind wasn't on it. Finally, he brought the meeting to a close by suggesting Callum take the men out in the land rover to see some of the places reserved for their clients. Everyone shook hands with Rory and he was finally free to join the General.

Rory began, "Sorry to keep you waiting."

"No, I'm sorry for intruding, but this couldn't wait," he handed over the envelope. "This is bad news Rory, best you be prepared."

Rory sat down and tore the envelope open. He read quickly and in disbelief. "No, oh no!" he cried, "She's left me! Why oh, why? I love her." He turned sharply on the General, "Why couldn't you have stopped her? When did she go?" By now, he was on his feet and pacing the tiny room.

The General stood up and grabbed his arm, "Sit down," he commanded, "I'll tell you all, I know," and Rory sat down. He was white, the General noticed. "Flame was sent a letter. Her War Office work was finished. The rent on her flat was to stop being paid. She was offered a flight home to France," he hesitated. "She told me she could see no future in your relationship because you wouldn't leave your wife."

Rory exploded, "I would have done," but the General waved his hand and continued. "She said you made it plain Rory, you didn't want to end your marriage. All she could see were years as your mistress and Pierre not having a proper father in his life. What were you thinking?" he had to ask.

Rory sprang up again, "She knew I loved her, both of them. Where is she? I have to talk to her."

"She left yesterday Rory, on a flight back to France. I am sorry. I did try to talk to her. I love her too. She's the daughter, I never had. Now she's gone, you will have to accept it, as will I. It was her decision."

"Oh no, I can't believe she'd do this to us!" Rory cried.

"Then again, I'm sorry. I'll leave you now but I'll come back in a few days, so we can talk some more. I'll leave you my card. Ring me, if you need me." The General place a card on the table, "Bye Rory" he patted his shoulder as he left.

Two hours later when Callum waved goodbye to their clients the office was closed and there was no sign of Rory. Now what, he frowned? And what had the General got to do with it? Callum swore darkly.

Chapter 18

Rory was missing for three days this time. When Callum found he still hadn't returned the morning after the General's visit he again rang Hamish. Whilst waiting for Hamish to arrive, Callum found Bonny and saw to her again. "You poor thing," he chatted to the bewildered dog. "Rory's got to stop doing this to you!"

Hamish arrived unable to believe Rory was missing yet again! The two telephoned Caitlyn in Inverness, (it was a working day for her) but she had no idea where he was. Hamish had also noticed Rory's car was missing. "I'm concerned he may have had an accident Callum. I'll ring the police—again!" This time Inspector Harris decided as it was only overnight that Rory had been gone, he would make inquiries before coming out to High Tor. "I'll keep you informed, Mr McGregor," he promised.

Hamish and Callum were left shaken. Where was Rory this time?

Once the General had left him, Rory sat in total shock. Flame had left him, returned to France! She hadn't even told him, just gone. She had taken his son with her, taken Pierre! The pain nearly did for him, sheer agony, twisting his gut. His mind was tormenting him with her words, written in the letter. 'You have a wife Rory, who you say you cannot leave', 'the guilt you are feeling over me will eventually break us up' and the most agonising 'Pierre deserves more of you than brief interludes in his life'. She had ended with her love, forever. She thanked him for his love and for giving her Pierre. She insisted, it was best to make a clean break now.

In utter dismay, Rory finally decided to visit the flat in Edinburgh. He drove like a wild man only to find the flat cold and empty. It was the truth, she was gone. Desolation swept over him. He couldn't bear the pain, nor could he stay here where her very presence haunted him. He staggered outside and seeing a public house on the corner, he craved a whisky. Once he started drinking he carried on. One pub followed another until he'd wandered further away from the flat and he was lost. Not that he cared one bit.

On the third morning, he was rudely awoken by a voice ten times louder in his head than pain allowed. "Mr Rory McGregor, I presume."

Rory opened bloodshot eyes and stared in utter confusion at a police constable. "We've been looking for you, Mr McGregor. Please come with me." He roughly 'assisted' Rory out of a grubby bed in a down town boarding house.

Rory stared around him. He had no idea how he came to be here, nor why his clothes were in such a filthy state. He did remember Flame had gone and tears ran down his cheek, "She's gone," he told the policeman. "Has she?" the policeman shook his head. Seeing the state Rory was in, he didn't blame her!

At the police station, a Sergeant asked him to confirm his name then decided, "Put him in a cell to sober up. I'll ring his father."

When Hamish arrived at the police station, he stared at Rory in disbelief. Minutes later, he was dragging Rory through a hotel lobby and into a bedroom. There was no way he could take his son home in this condition. It would give Isla the fright of her life! Next moment, he had stripped Rory and pushed him under a shower. "Clean yourself up, you stink like a pig," he scolded.

Once Rory was clean again and wrapped in a towel, Hamish ordered black coffee and lots of it please, to be sent to his room. When it arrived, he insisted Rory start drinking it whilst he rang Callum.

"Hallo Callum. Rory has turned up and I could do with your help. How are you fixed?"

"Of course, I'll help. What do you need? How is he?" he stammered.

"Not too good. Firstly, could you let my wife know he's been found and I'll be bringing him home soon? Secondly Rory needs clean clothes, everything you understand? Could you bring them here to us?" He read out the hotel address.

"Yes, I can do that. Is there anything else?"

"No, that's it. I'm very grateful to you Callum, thanks," he hung up.

Hamish turned to Rory, who was looking slightly better and nodded, "Good, now I think you've some explaining to do." He sat down on the edge of the bed, "And we aren't leaving here until I'm satisfied you've told me everything."

Rory groaned softly. He was feeling awful and all the events of the past few days were flooding back. He could feel the pain of losing Flame all over again. He groaned again. "No Dad, believe me, you don't want to know," he insisted. Next moment, he stretched out on the bed. Hamish stared in disbelief. He had no idea how to deal with this. Next minute Rory was fast asleep.

Callum's arrival disturbed Rory. His head was bursting but he felt a little better. "What are you doing here?" he asked Callum rudely.

"Callum has kindly brought you some clean clothes," Hamish snapped at him. "I suggest you get into them." Reluctantly, Rory got off the bed, his head swimming and began dressing. In truth, he appreciated the fresh clothes.

"Thanks for bringing these, Callum," he muttered.

Hamish had ordered fresh coffee and some sandwiches. "Help yourself Callum, you too Rory. You'll feel better with some food inside you then we must talk," he demanded. He shook his head, "I'm ashamed of you Rory, to think I found you," but Rory snapped, "No Dad, don't."

"It has to be said. Perhaps if Callum hears what state you were in, it may bring you to your senses," he turned to Callum, "Rory was in a doss house completely incapable. He ended up in a police cell. I've never seen him so drunk," he held up a beer stained shirt for him to see, "I've had to bail him out of a police station."

"Why?" Callum was shocked. "Oh Rory, what is it. What's wrong?"

"That is what I want to find out," Hamish nodded, "So you either start talking now, or when we get home. Do you want to explain to your mother?"

Rory was shaken. He shook his head knowing he was beaten. He couldn't fight any longer. "Okay, perhaps you're right, it is time I talked, but you may not like what you hear. Remember, you forced me to tell you." He made himself comfortable, sitting on the bed and poured another cup of coffee, "It's a long story and it begins the night I went missing. By the way this is still officially top secret. That night I drove an agent out onto the moors, miles away to a valley where I found an airstrip." Hamish gasped.

"Did you say an airstrip, on our land?"

"Yes on the fringes anyway. To cut a long story short, the agent became ill, really sick and stupidly, I took his place."

"You did what?" asked Callum and Hamish simply gasped, neither had any idea about any of this.

"All I had to do was unload the supplies for the French Resistance once we landed in France and return home, but there was no one there to meet us, so I had to get out, hide the goods and wait for the French to arrive. They didn't come, instead the Germans arrived, and I was arrested. They naturally assumed I was a spy!" By now Hamish and Callum were in shock, unable to speak.

"I was locked in a cell for a few days, expecting to be shot at any moment. On the fourth night a woman arrived, in uniform and speaking German to take me to Paris for questioning. Once outside, she spoke French. She was Resistance and had come to rescue me. We hid in a cellar. I owe her my life, Dad and whilst there, we became lovers. I was moved on from there and flown home," he paused for a drink. By now, Hamish and Callum were hanging on to his every word. Rory continue, "The reason I was captured was because Flame's cell, that was the girl's code name, had a traitor and he'd tipped off the Germans about the drop. Long after I left Flame discovered his identity and he shot her."

"Oh no, Rory," Callum cried shocked, "But how do you know all this?"

"Flame was flown out of France and into hospital in Edinburgh, seriously hurt. Whilst there she had a baby, my baby, my son," Rory whispered.

"Oh no Rory, I find this hard to believe," gasped Hamish, "You're telling me you've a son?" Rory stared at him and nodded, "It's true"

"This is the French girl, the English lessons," Callum worked out in disbelief.

Rory smiled, "Yes and I made a good job of it too. The lessons were organised by the General, that part was true."

"Are you telling me you've been having an affair with this girl? I'm disgusted Rory. You are married and have responsibilities at High Tor. This has to end," Hamish snapped.

Rory practically ignore him, "Last week, the General came to see me. He brought me a letter. Now the war is over Flame loses her flat and provisions from the War Office. They offered her a flight home and she took it. I have lost the only woman I'll ever love and my son, hence my drunken spree."

"She has gone—back to France?" Hamish asked, "Good riddance to them both. I doubt the child was even yours."

Rory's eyes blazed, "How dare you! He was your grandson too and probably the only one you'll ever have!"

"Don't talk rubbish—you and Caitlyn will have– one day," he stammered.

"We're finished after this. I refuse to live a lie any longer. Caitlyn will be twice as happy to be free of me. Oh! And yes, Caitlyn never wants children, so you can forget that too," Rory shouted. Everyone was silent then Rory sighed, "I warned you Dad, not to push me into explaining all this, but now you know I'm not sorry. It's a relief to me to have it all out in the open." He stood up and went to the mini bar in the room and took out a whisky. Callum moved quickly and took Rory's arm, "That's not the answer mate." He took the bottle and turned to Hamish. "More coffee I think" he asked and Hamish nodded. Callum rang room service and ordered another tray.

Callum poured it this time. He asked Hamish, "What happens now?"

"I'll take him home with me and give him time to dry out. To be honest, I'm utterly lost. It's as if I don't know my own son," he admitted.

"I am here," Rory snapped.

Callum shook his head, "Rory," he whispered, "If only we'd known what you've been through."

"I couldn't tell you," he sighed. "You'll never know how many times, I wanted to tell you Callum."

Callum crossed the room swiftly to hug his friend and suddenly Rory broke down. He held onto Callum desperately as tears fell. It was just what Rory needed. "I'm so sorry about Caitlyn," he whispered when he calmed down.

"We'll sort it out, I promise," Callum assured him. "Would you like me to explain everything to her?"

Rory shook his head, "You can't tell her or anyone else. I warned you, all this is covered by the Official Secrets Act."

Now Hamish was worried, "What do I tell your mother? She has to be told."

Rory grinned, "Now you both know how it feels to evade questions all the time. It never ends, and you end up telling people lies."

Hamish looked completely lost, "So what do I do?" he asked helplessly.

Rory shook his head, "You better ring the General and explain the fix we're in. I could be in trouble over this—as well as getting drunk!" He searched his wallet for the card, the General had given him.

The General insisted he'd join them at the hotel. Whilst they waited Rory again stretched out on the bed to nurse a blinding headache. He swore he'd never drink again.

The General quickly summed up the situation. "I am sorry but not surprised. Rory has been under so much stress for so long, something had to give and losing Flame broke him." He ignored a scowl from Hamish. "So now you both know but no one else can be told. This cannot be made common knowledge."

"But we have to tell his mother—and his wife," Hamish insisted.

"No, I mean no one," the General shook his head firmly. "However, I suggest you tell them Rory has had a mistress and a son who have returned to France now, the war is over." He nodded, "They don't need to know the rest anyway. I'm sure telling them that will be enough of a shock anyway."

Callum nodded, "Yes, I believe that would work."

"Maybe, but is all this secrecy still needed now the war is over?" Hamish demanded.

"Very much so, people's lives could depend on it. Take Flame for example. Even now, there will be Germans trying to discover her identity and take their revenge on her," the General told them.

Silence fell as this was thought about by them all. It was Callum who broke it, "I can understand a lot more now. I'll not speak about any of it."

"No, nor will I," Hamish agreed. "We'll simply say Rory had a French mistress. Thank you General, we desperately needed your help here."

"I'm pleased to have been of assistance." He turned to Rory, "I ought to report this, but I won't. Promise me, no more drunken sprees."

Rory nodded, embarrassed, "I promise. I am sorry for this General. We all appreciate your help."

"I'll come over and see you one day soon," the General promised, then shook hands all round and he left.

"Let's go home," Hamish stood up and asked Rory, "Where's your car?"

"At Flame's flat," he suddenly remembered.

"Well, you can't drive in your state. We'll have to leave it until tomorrow," he decided. He turned to Callum. "I am really grateful for all your help today. I am really sorry some of the revelations involved your sister though. I'd not have called on you, if I'd known."

"You had no more idea than me what today was all about, Mr McGregor, so there's no need for apologies. I'll get back to the office. I'll see you soon Rory, get some rest mate."

Hamish collected up Rory's dirty clothes and settled the bill at reception. He and Rory then drove home to Inverness, expecting fireworks in the coming days.

Chapter 19

After nearly a month in Paris, Flame was struggling. The city was overcrowded with people arriving daily, all looking for work and homes. Today Flame and Pierre were moving out of the small hotel that had been home to them since they arrived and into one room in a down town house. Money was now short and she had no hope of work in the near future. Flame cared little for herself, hadn't her life been tough at times, but she cared about Pierre. If only she could find work, any work but as soon as people saw Pierre they turned her down. After scrubbing and cleaning everything in the room and feeding Pierre, the two set out again, looking for work.

The room was in a poorer area of Paris but Flame hoped with more opportunities of finding work. There were some shops close by and she began asking there. The first few told her outright they didn't need anyone but in a corner shop selling groceries, an elderly woman looked closely at Flame and asked, "What did you do before?"

"I have been home having my baby," she replied.

"Where is your husband?" came next.

"My husband died Madame. He was English. Pierre and I are alone."

The woman nodded, "I'm getting old. I need an early morning cleaner for the shop, 6 a.m. to 7:30 six days a week. I can't pay much (she named a small amount). It's up to you."

Flame nodded, "Thank you Madame, but I'd need to bring Pierre with me." She held her breath.

"I assumed you would. I'll not object if the work gets done. My name is Rene Rousseau."

"Thank you Madame, I accept. When shall I start?" Flame beamed.

"Tomorrow and don't be late or you're out."

"Yes Madame, I'll be here." Flame was elated. This was enough to pay the rent on the room with a little to spare. She would still need a second job to be safe but it was a start, a good omen, she decided.

Flame settled into the new routine and worked hard for Madame each day. At first Madame was sharp, watching over her but gradually she relaxed leaving Flame to work alone. She paid her regularly and in time found items from the shop for Flame to take home as well.

Often tired and lonely at night, Flame sometimes regretted leaving Edinburgh. At least, there she'd have had a home, food and Rory but her stubborn pride refused to let her be a 'kept woman'. Both she and Pierre deserved more than that but oh, how she missed Rory. He never left her thoughts, never left her yearning for his body close at night. Such thoughts had her waking in the early hours hot and frustrated. However, she knew she'd made the decision herself and for the right reasons. She simply had to get on with it.

Flame made a breakthrough one morning as September turned into October. Pierre had developed a harsh cough and Flame was worried. She saved up enough to pay for a doctor's appointment. She was sitting in the doctor's waiting room when two women sitting beside her began a conversation. One was sounding as desperate as Flame for money. She asked the second woman, "I don't suppose you know of any jobs going?"

"As a matter of fact, I do," the second woman replied and Flame's hearing was on full alert. "Edith Models is expanding. They are recruiting on Friday. Can you use a machine?"

The second woman said she could and added, "Oh, thank you so much. I'll go along early on Friday."

"So will I," decided Flame, straight after I've cleaned the shop. She'd have to take bread for Pierre to eat whilst they waited. She had used a sewing machine to make her own clothes in the convent, surely that counted? Next moment she was called in to see the doctor, who assured her Pierre would recover well that the cough was nothing serious. He gave her a bottle of cough linctus.

Friday morning found Flame queuing outside a large warehouse, along with lots of other women. What chance did she have, she fretted with all these women here and her with a child?

However, she moved slowly forward towards the entrance, deciding to at least try!

Finally, Flame made it inside the lobby after an exhausting wait. She was just starring around to see where to go next, when a man moved towards her.

"Well I never, it is you! I never expected to see you again," he exclaimed.

Bemused Flame stared at him in amazement, "Gervaise!"

"The one and only, oh it's good to see you," he smiled happily, "Look, can we talk somewhere more private?"

Torn Flame hesitated, "I really need some work. I don't want to lose my place."

He grinned again, "Oh, I think I can find you some work. Accountancy, am I right?"

"Can you?" Flame was shaking. Could it be true? What was he doing here?

"Come to my office," Gervaise invited, "Who is this young man?" He took her arm and led her to a smart carpeted room on the first floor. Flame followed blindly, totally confused. "Take a seat and relax. I assure you this is all above board. It's a long story but my wife owns this place and I'm the managing director."

"You are—she does?" she stammered.

Gervaise had quickly summed up, Flame was in a bad way. She was thin and pale and poorly dressed. He decided to give her a few minutes to herself, time to compose herself. "I'm just going to order us some coffee. What would the young man like to drink—would milk do?" Flame nodded, "Thank you."

When the coffee tray arrived, it was loaded with a plate piled high with buttered croissants as well as coffee and milk.

Flame's mouth watered at such luxury. Gervaise was pleased, he'd done something to help her. "Please help yourselves. It's my one weakness each morning." Flame took one and handed it to Pierre.

"So, Flame—what is you real name, its best I don't call you Flame around here," he worried. She told him Yvette.

"What's been happening to you?" he wondered.

Suddenly, Flame's eyes filled with tears. For weeks she'd lived amongst strangers, people who didn't know her or care about her. Now here was Gervaise who knew her well, knew what she's been through and it all came tumbling out. Meanwhile Pierre was having a feast of croissants and loving it!

Gervaise listened quietly, letting her talk. He was shocked to hear she'd been shot by Yves and that he was the traitor. When she told him, Bear had flown her out to Scotland, he'd nodded. Thank God he had! This was one of the bravest women he'd ever met. She had fought for France but now look at her, he thought sadly. He was so glad he was in a position to help her. He'd have to do it without hurting her pride though.

"Well it's your lucky day. We are expanding the factory and need new staff in all departments. We need new accountants. Are you interested?"

"Yes, I am, oh thank you," Flame said quietly. Gervaise filled in her name and address on a form. He knew the area she now lived in and his heart sank. "That's fine. I'll forward it to the department for you."

"I'm worried, Gervaise. What about Pierre whilst I work," she whispered, still afraid all this was a dream.

"I was coming to that, but first, I'd like to tell you what happened to us when we left Villenue. We got to Paris safely, to my wife's brother and his wife, but we knew eventually the Germans would trace us to them and we were putting them in danger. However, they insisted we stayed and they moved us into their attic. We lived there out of sight and no one ever knew we were there. They saved our lives. Now to what's happening today. My brother in law owned this factory but sadly, he died recently. His widow inherited it, but she is seriously ill, and my wife nurses her. My sister in law is too ill to run it, so she has signed it over to my wife," he paused wondering if Flame had followed all that. "Now I've a suggestion, why don't you and Pierre move into the attic? It's big, furnished and has a bathroom. We were very comfortable up there and when you start working for us, Edith my wife would love to babysit Pierre." He held his breath, would she agree? Flame sat silent, what did she say to such a wonderful offer. She smiled at last, "Yes please," she agreed.

Chapter 20

Life at High Tor was in uproar. Rory had moved back permanently into the Stables and now lived alone, apart from Bonny. Caitlyn was spitting fire and filing for divorce. She was asking for settlements galore from Rory. She even claimed money out of the House. If she won, High Tor couldn't survive in its current state. Fortunately, Hamish stood firm over the House. He was still its owner, not Rory, so she had no claim.

However, Hamish and Isla were not standing by Rory. No one divorced in their family, no matter what. What Rory had done was unforgiveable in their eyes. They agreed with Caitlyn and expected him to grovel to Caitlyn and repair their marriage. Rory simply refused. The rift between him and his parents was so wide, he wondered if it could ever be breached. He lived quietly, worked hard and walked the moors with Bonny. High Tor House stood empty and cold as if it too was in mourning. He was so grateful he and Caitlyn had never moved in there.

Callum continued to work closely with Rory, something Rory felt guilty about. What an awful position for him to be in, torn between his sister and his friend. However, it was Callum himself who assured Rory he wouldn't give up on a lifetime friendship, over this. He did ask not to be involved though.

Callum was in the Stables office on the day the divorce papers arrived from Caitlyn's solicitors. Rory read them silently but as the claims mounted he turned white with anger and Callum couldn't help asking. "What is it Rory?"

"The divorce papers—please don't worry. I'll sort it," Rory replied embarrassed.

Callum had been warned by Morag not to get involved, but if he was honest he had strong views on his sister. Now he couldn't ignore Rory's distress and leant over and picked up the paperwork, ignoring Rory's "No!"

What he read had him incensed, "Oh no, Rory—you can't—it's wrong," he gasped.

Rory lay back in his chair and whispered, "It will cripple High Tor, we may lose farms—workers," he groaned, "But as I'm continually told, it's my fault and Caitlyn has every right to do this."

"What will you do?" Callum asked. He was horrified.

"The only thing, I can do is take it to my solicitor. He will try to reduce the amounts. I'm sorry Callum, Caitlyn is your sister and I admit I've treated her badly, but I never hurt her intentionally. Things happened in France and I fell in love. I handled everything badly and now I'm reaping the consequences. Only trouble is, so is High Tor."

"I don't know what to say," Callum sighed. He handed back the papers. "I believe you and I'm so sorry for you."

Rory nodded and tried to resume work on the forms, they'd been dealing with.

That evening, Callum tried to talk to his mother about Rory. She didn't really want to listen. Caitlyn was again staying in Inverness.

Callum insisted. "Have you any idea of the demands Caitlyn is making in the divorce settlement?"

"No, but surely as the injured party she is entitled to compensation."

"Today, I saw her solicitor's letter to Rory. If Caitlyn gets all she wants then High Tor is finished as we know it. Rory will have to sell off half of it and we and many others will be out."

"No, Rory would never sell Beacon Farm!" Morag gasped.

"Think about it Mum, which of the farms here would bring in the most cash? Ours without doubt and if I was Rory this farm would go before the House."

"Oh Callum," Morag cried, shaken, "But if Caitlyn is due compensation," she stammered.

"There's compensation and downright greed. I know she's family but I reckon she's bleeding him dry, just because she can," he hesitated, "And we both know she's not as pure as she makes out."

"Is there anything, we can do?" Morag fretted. Even now she couldn't condemn her own daughter.

"I'm thinking Mum. If I 'interfere' as you call it, how much could it hurt Cat? If I do nothing, how many of us up here will lose our farms and livelihoods?"

"What can you do though?" Morag asked, "Oh, I can't think, this is awful. At times I could strangle Caitlyn," tears fell down her face, "I've always loved Rory, ever since he was a little boy, but what he's done—it's disgraceful. I don't know what to tell you to do, son, but if you can do anything to save us—then best you do it."

"Thanks Mum," Callum got up and hugged his Mum. *I'll sleep on things*, he decided.

Next morning, Callum turned up at the Stables office to be greeted by Rory, "Hallo, I didn't expect to see you this morning. Have I forgotten something?"

"No, you haven't; in fact, I'm not here about business today, I've come about Caitlyn," he held up a hand, "No, please listen to me, let me get this said."

Rory sat back surprised. He waited, sensing Callum was upset, "I've something for you, information that will put Caitlyn in the wrong. It will help you fight her claims, but it will hurt her, especially knowing it's me who told you what I've done."

"Done what, Callum?" Rory was sitting up listening intently.

Callum handed over a large envelope. "A while back, I had a go at Caitlyn about her life style in Inverness. She scorned me, said I didn't have a life whilst she did and nothing I said made any difference to her. I told mum what I suspected, but she wouldn't listen to me either," he sighed. "I admit, I was angry and I decided to find out just what Cat got up to in Inverness and Edinburgh. In truth, I was worried about her Rory, she is my sister. I hired a private detective. I've never told mum by the way. This is his report and you are welcome to it. I just hope exposing her, helps you and High Tor." Without another word, he got up and left, leaving a bewildered Rory staring at the envelope.

Rory picked the envelope up and stared at it, for a moment, before opening it. What he read shocked him. It was a detailed account of Caitlyn's night life. There were photos of her on the arms of different men. There were names of men, dates and times, including the places they met. Nowhere, did it actually say she was sleeping around but if she was capable of this, it followed she was.

Rory's numbness gave way to white hot anger. How dare Caitlyn! When he remembered how hard he'd tried to make her happy. He'd even given in when she wanted to return to work, now he felt a fool. She had manipulated him for her own pleasure. Well, she was in for a shock! When his solicitor saw this, he'd put an end to her claims. She'd be lucky to get even a penny out of him.

Rory saw to the essential paperwork waiting for him then closed up early. He and Bonny headed out over the moors. Slowly Rory's temper subsided, and he suddenly thought of Callum. What must it have cost him to expose his sister's behaviour to him? He wondered if Morag had seen the report by now. If she had, he couldn't imagine the pain she was feeling. The question he now asked himself was could he make the report common knowledge? Oh, he'd love every moment of Caitlyn's shame, revenge would be so sweet, but what about Callum and Morag? Did they deserve to be hurt because of Caitlyn's behaviour? He decided for their sakes alone to think this through calmly. He settled down by a stream and watched a kingfisher dive for fish. What a mess he'd made of his life, most of it by his own hand. Flame was still with him, she never left but she might as well be on the moon for all the good remembering her did. Why had he kept her hidden? If he'd been open from the start she'd still be here, he groaned. Darkness was falling when he eventually returned to the Stables. He still hadn't made any decisions about the papers, he grinned. That was the story of his life.

Rory slept surprisingly well that night and woke early next morning, realising at some point in the night he'd found a solution. He rang Callum, "Is Caitlyn at home?" he wondered.

"Yes, she's here, she arrived last night but she's still in bed," Callum told him. What now, he wondered?

"Right, I'd like to come over and see her. Ask her to get dressed as I need to talk to her. You as well Callum," he decided last minute.

Callum agreed and turned to his Mum. "Rory's coming to talk to Caitlyn, to me too," he told her.

"So you—did, what Callum?"

"I will tell you later Mum, though, you might not like it. For now, could you get Caitlyn up?" Callum asked her and she agreed.

Rory arrived before Caitlyn was up. Things were difficult between him and Morag, so greetings were strained. "If you'd like to wait in the sitting room, I'll get you a coffee," she told him and Rory thanked her. Callum followed him in and the two settled down. Nothing was said, it was an embarrassing wait until Caitlyn appeared and Morag returned to the kitchen.

Rory studied Caitlyn as she walked in. Obviously, she had no idea about the report, as she was smug and confident. Maybe, he'd get some revenge after all, Rory smiled.

"I guess you've come to discuss the divorce?" she began.

"I have Caitlyn, I'm here to ask you to drop all your claims," Rory told her straight.

Caitlyn gasped, "You want—are you joking? Why on earth would I do that?"

"To save yourself from having your name dragged into the gutter," Rory advised her and continued, "I have here, a detective's report on your—disgusting behaviour in Inverness and Edinburgh. Have a look if you don't believe me." He handed over the envelope. Caitlyn snatched it up and began reading it. "You put a private eye on me? How could you?" she accused Rory.

"No, not Rory, me, I did it Cat. I tried to talk to you. I suspected what he found out– How could you do that?" Callum pointed to the paperwork.

"You've ruined everything Callum, can't you see that. I was set up for life with this settlement. I'm ruined now," Caitlyn screamed at her brother.

"You appear to have done that all by yourself," Rory insisted. "So now, we have to decide where we go from here. I assume you don't want this read out in court, photos printed in the newspapers for all to see?"

Caitlyn turned white, "You wouldn't do that. Oh no, you won't, will you?"

"Oh, I would Caitlyn. I have admitted to adultery but you— you've lied to everyone, insisting you're whiter than white and that I've ruined your life. Yet, all the time you've been selling yourself to the highest bidder"

"I never—it wasn't like that"

"Right, cards on the table, drop all your claims and we'll settle on an amicable divorce. I'll pay you a one-off payment and I'll burn this report," Rory spoke sharply.

"You can't do that. You kept a mistress, my solicitor says I'm entitled to a decent pay-out," Caitlyn cried.

Rory nodded, "Fair enough Cat, I'm more than happy to give this to my solicitor. I don't know why I tried to save your reputation after all you've done. We'll have to fight this out in court, it's your decision." He stood up and collected the papers.

"No, no, wait, let me think," Caitlyn begged frantically. "How much will you give me?" she demanded.

"We can decide on that later. I'll ask my dad to mediate for us. It will be fair, I promise," Rory assured her.

"Okay, I've no choice, have I?" Caitlyn realised she was beaten.

"No, not really," Rory actually grinned this time.

"And you promise me you'll burn those?" she pointed to the envelope, now firmly held by Rory.

"I will, when the divorce is final, Caitlyn. If you double cross me in the meantime, they go to my solicitor."

"You are being cruel, Rory," Caitlyn sulked.

"I am, but only because you forced me into this. Do you realise, I'd have had to sell High Tor to raise the money you were demanding. Your mum could have been left without the farm," he told her. "I'll leave you now and wait to hear from your solicitor."

"I'll see you out," Callum stood up too and followed Rory out.

Once outside Callum sighed deeply. "Oh, thank you for sparing her Rory. You handled that well."

"It's me that owes you a massive debt of gratitude, Callum. You've saved High Tor and I'll never be able to repay you." Rory was trembling.

"Then I'd say we're quits mate," Callum laughed and the two hugged.

"Thanks Callum, now I better go and tell my parents the good news," Rory decided.

"Are things any better between you?"

"Not really, oh I can understand, but honestly, wouldn't you think they'd at least meet me half way?" Rory sighed. "Perhaps, in time they'll come round." He got into his car and waved goodbye. A huge weight had lifted from him and at last he felt a glimmer of hope.

Chapter 21

Rory was busy in the office again the next morning. His paperwork load had increased since the end of the war. There were so many forms to sign to close agreements with the Ministry of Agriculture. He was surprised and pleased to answer the phone and find the General on the other end.

"Good morning Rory, how are you?" he asked and Rory said 'fine'. "Can I come over and see you today?" he wondered.

"Of course, you can. Have you news of Flame?" he fretted.

"No sorry, not this time. I'll come on over," he decided and an hour later, he arrived.

Rory offered him a coffee and asked, "So what is so urgent today, not that I'm not pleased to see you?" he asked once they were both settled with drinks.

"It has come to London's ears that you are getting divorced. I've been asked to talk to you. I'm to tell you from them, that at no point must France and the Resistance be mentioned in the proceedings. I'm afraid you are still bound by the official secrets act."

Rory was stunned. He gazed at the General and asked, "How on earth do they know? Am I being watched even now?"

"No, nothing as bad as that, but they have ways and means for finding out these things, that's all I'll say. I've passed on their message, so my job's done. You can now tell me all about it," he smiled and Rory relaxed. He liked the General and was happy to have someone to listen to him.

"You can tell London not to worry. As far as the divorce is concerned, I'm charged with adultery with a French girl named Yvette, nothing more. In fact, the divorce should go through unchallenged," Rory explained.

"That's good, I'm glad for you. So, how are you coping?"

"How do you think? My marriage is over and I've lost friends and family because of my affair. And the worse of it is I've lost the only woman, I'll ever love and my son." Rory snapped, "Sorry, it's all so hard. Do you know how Flame is?" he begged.

"I'm sorry Rory. I've heard nothing since she left. I asked her to keep in touch and I'm a little concerned," he admitted. In fact, he was getting more than concerned as the weeks passed. "I promise I'll tell you how she is if I hear, but I can't give you her address at any time, because I agreed not to."

Rory believed him but knowing he too was worried about Flame didn't help. The two continued talking for quite a while before the General left. Rory had enjoyed his visit.

How strange life was the General thought, when on returning home he found a letter from Flame. He opened it eagerly. She wrote, I have settled down at last, in Paris with a family I knew in the past. Pierre and I have a flat to ourselves and I am working as an accountant. We are both well and we would love to see you if you care to visit. There's plenty of room in the flat for you to stay with us. Our address is (She included it). Do come, she ended. Well, well, smiled the General, I'm coming Flame. He couldn't wait to see her again and to pass on the latest news from High Tor.

The divorce dragged on slowly, but Rory accepted that, the law always moved slowly. In the meantime, he decided to move back into High Tor House. He engaged his dad to help him and as the two worked closely together, a good relationship developed again. The day he moved in permanently, he threw a small celebratory tea and his parents both came along as did Morag and Callum. Caitlyn was again working full time in Inverness on the magazine. She had moved in with her friend and only occasionally came home to High Tor. She told her mum that all the escort business was now behind her. She had learnt her lesson and looked forward to one day buying a house in Inverness. In the end, it was a happy day and as if to endorse it, that evening Rory received a phone call from the General to tell him he'd actually seen Flame and she and Pierre were well. Rory thanked him sincerely. It was good to know they were well, even if the knowledge was bitter sweet.

The day the divorce was finalised there were no celebrations for Rory. His life was a mess and he'd lost Flame forever. As for his son, he mourned his loss daily. He didn't see Caitlyn. Instead, his dad met up with her and handed over a cheque for the agreed settlement. He also gave her the envelope from the private eye. He told her, "Rory thought you should have this to destroy yourself. That way, you'll know it's gone for good." Caitlyn sent her thanks for it to Rory.

One month later, the General arrived at the House unannounced. "Have you time for a chat Rory?" he wondered.

"Of course, anytime, was there something in particular?" he asked.

"Yes, there is and I'm hoping it is good news for you, after all this time," he grinned. "I hear the divorce is final?"

"Yes, it's all over and no mention of France, you can assure London."

"Good, well you'll be pleased to hear I've just returned from France again—and yes, I saw Flame," he smiled. "I explained that your divorce was going through and she sent you a letter, to be given to you, once it was final." Out of his pocket, he took an envelope and handed it over.

"Oh General, what can I say? Thank you is so inadequate," Rory's eyes shone.

"You can promise me one thing Rory. Flame is the closest I'll ever have to a daughter and to see her hurt by you was heart-breaking. If you ever hurt her again, I won't be responsible for my actions," he insisted.

"You have my word," Rory nodded, "Does that mean—does she want to see me?" he could hardly breathe.

"It's all in the letter. Flame is making no promises. She is simply willing to meet up again. Oh yes, and I have to be there too," he added with a grin.

Rory was trembling, could it be true? He couldn't speak.

"Nothing to say, that's a first," the General chuckled. "In my humble opinion, Flame is still very much in love with you and as for you, I don't need to ask. I am assured, when two people love one another, love does find a way. So, the only question now is when we can leave for France?"

Rory threw himself into the General's arms and shed a few tears, "Thank you so much, for everything," he sobbed. Later that night, Rory and Callum sat in the drawing room of the House drinking bottles of beer. Callum was almost as excited as Rory by the news. He assured Rory he couldn't wait to meet Flame. Earlier Rory had visited his parents and told them he'd be leaving for Paris in a few days. Callum would take over the Estates.

"Will you be bringing her home straight away?" Isla wanted to know. Rory had no idea, "If I do, will you make her welcome?" he demanded and Isla blushed. "I'll certainly try Rory," she replied stiffly and Rory had to be satisfied.

It was Hamish who offered to drive Rory and the General to the airport. He had not said much about Rory going to see his 'French girl' but as they walked through to boarding, he took Rory's arm and pulled him to one side. "I just need to say this Rory before you leave. I once wished you'd find someone you could love with a fierce passion, just like I did with your mother. It seems to me my wish has been granted. Go and be happy with Yvette, Rory. I can't wait to meet her and my grandson. I assure you they will both be made welcome at High Tor."

Rory hugged his dad, "Oh Dad! That means everything to me. Thank you."

"Time to go, Rory," the General called and together they boarded the plane.

When they reached France, Flame and Pierre were waiting impatiently for their arrival. Rory swung Pierre up into his arms and clasped Flame awkwardly holding them both close. He couldn't believe it was actually happening after so long.

They spent the time sight-seeing for the first few days, both awkward and cautious with each other, until one evening the General sent them out for a meal alone together, whilst he cared for Pierre. They ordered drinks and a meal, before Rory told her, "The General wants me to talk," he admitted, "But the last thing I want to do is rush into anything."

"I'm happy to listen," Flame told him.

Rory nodded, "Okay. I'll begin by admitting, I've been thinking a lot over the past months Flame. I realise I've had a privileged life in many ways. I've drifted along without thought a lot of the time and that was true of the night I got on that plane. It was the most idiotic thing to do, but my actions had a catastrophic effect on so many people. My stupidity put so many people in danger, especially you. In the cellar it continued, I did the unforgiveable, I slept with you. Oh, I loved you so much too but to sleep with you with no thought for the consequences, I'm so ashamed Flame."

Flame's hand came across the table and gripped his. "There's nothing to forgive. I was a more than willing partner, don't forget."

"You were, I admit," he laughed, "But Flame, having fallen in love with you, when I got home, I allowed Caitlyn to persuade me into marrying her! I drifted into it again, didn't I? When unbelievably you came back into my life in Edinburgh, the joy I felt was exquisite but instead of owning up and acknowledging you and Pierre, I began a secret life with you because it was easy to do. I was such a coward and I hurt you so badly. I can't begin to put things right with you. It even took you leaving to blow everything out in the open. Even then I didn't stand up and confess to my parents and wife." He had to stop for a moment as their meals arrived. It gave him a chance to catch his breath too.

Flame was still holding his hand. "You don't need to put yourself through this Rory."

"Oh, I do. I've made such a mess of everything and I can't excuse my behaviour. Now, I've forced myself to face the truth, I am hoping somehow, I'll be a better person in future. The immediate problem is, I am still in love with you Flame and Pierre is the one joy of my life. I'll forever thank God for him. I don't deserve it, but can you find a way for me to be part of your lives?"

"Oh, I can Rory, quite easily," she smiled. "I don't believe I can live my life without you. As for Pierre, he already loves you and in years to come, he will need you. Have you any suggestions on how we can spend the rest of our lives together?"

The restaurant customers were quite surprised when two people suddenly sprung out of their seats and began to passionately kiss each other. Next moment, they simply shrugged and ignored them. After all, this was Paris!

Rory returned to High Tor one week later, to prepare his friends and family for his marriage to Flame in Paris. The General stayed with Flame, helping to sort out a marriage license and venues. Everyone was happy but he himself was over the moon, proud to have had a major part in bringing these two lovely people together.

One month later, a small party set out from Scotland. They were Rory and his parents and Callum and his mother. The wedding took place in Paris and was also attended by Gervaise and his family. Everyone agreed, it was a wonderful day.

Finally, Rory was able to bring his new bride home to High Tor, where according to legend; High Tor House was waiting to welcome a new bride.